When The Pilot Light Goes Out

DANIEL STONE

Who's Crying?
Fly away, like a bird pirouetting in the sky,
Break free, life's twisted, who wants to die?
I want to live forever, a memory, tear drops in her eye.
I want to be loved; whose love is not a lie?
I want to cry on shoulders, I want my problems heard.
I want my best friend right now to tell me I'm absurd,
I want to be that very bird pirouetting in the sky,
I don't want to live forever,
But I don't want to die,
I want to be that bird,
That bird will never cry.

Pilot light '96

1 – THE WORLD'S END

USING ONE HAND AND A KNEE, I once again raised the anchor and was reunited with Mason's head and body. The plastic bags were slimy and muddy on the outside but they had kept him dry on the inside, which was good. I fetched my fishing tackle bag and took out my maggot box; I didn't feel like fishing so I poured the contents, a pint of mixed grubs all different colours, into Mason's bag. His head and body came alive in a wriggling orgy. I sealed the bag again as best as I could and stored it under the bowels of the boat. I should have thought of doing that last night.

It was mid-morning, as light as it was going to get today: not very light at all. It was cloudy and grey and drizzly; even the starlings looked bored with the gloominess. Although I was shivering and yet burning-up, it was neither hot nor cold. It was England's temperate climate personified.

I was pleased to be leaving London, but totally numb and devoid of all other feelings and emotion. I guess that must have been the coke working. I'd been paranoid now I just felt free, liberated even. As I headed west, passing a large housing estate that backed onto the canal itself, I could have been in any number of countries and in any time over the last hundred years; only the discarded blue bags floating in the canal like man-made jelly fish gave away the year and country in which we were living. People's shit from expensive corner shops thrown away and now choking any hope of urban wildlife. I hated people I didn't even know; it was them, not me, and that was the problem. Angry head, possibly still the coke. I never purposely littered anything that wasn't biodegradable. I was a lot of things but I wasn't a litter bug.

As I silently cursed the world and its inhabitants my eyes checked the fuel gauge for the thousandth time. There was plenty; there always was, nothing changed – I just couldn't stop checking. I really didn't want to stop and refuel; too many questions, far too many people, and by keeping

1

my eyes in the boat I ignored any pedestrians on the bank. Maybe I needed more drugs. I stopped as I noticed I was running alongside the eerie Kensal Green cemetery. There were so many dead people. Would we one day cover the earth with coffins and graveyards? I wondered if any of my relations were in there; maybe they'd be turning in their graves to say hello or turn their backs on me in disgust.

My eyes were then drawn to the West Way Road that jutted over the canal like a giant concrete Scaletrix track. I imagined an old JPS Lotus racing car flying off the road and crashing into the canal and then a big kid's hand swooping out of the sky, putting the car back onto the road and sending it on its way. As I chugged on I could make out the towers of Wormwood Scrubs. I was close enough already; I certainly didn't want to be any closer.

Acton Lane Power station straddles the hell holes know as Harlesden and Willesden. Why I hated them I don't know, but I didn't like them at all; an irrational hatred, a bit like my feelings towards tomatoes, Robbie Williams, Tottenham and people picking their nose in public. The canal crossed the North Circular Road on a large aqueduct; I marvelled at the strange contrast between the million-miles-an-hour Sunday rat race, the constant stream of people in their cars, and the chilled-out four-miles-per-hour canal way of life, just drifting along almost at nature's pace. There was a traffic jam and my four mile per hour was currently getting me home quicker than those stuck on the road. I laughed uncontrollably until I cried. I don't know why I laughed or cried, perhaps I died.

The canal continued west through Alperton and Greenford. I only knew this because I was looking at the Grand Union Canal route planner I was using as a guide that was open in front of me on the boat's cockpit. Occasionally my eyes shuddered, I guessed due to fatigue. The surrounding area was mostly flat, but Horesden Hill and Perivale Wood provided a long stretch of beautiful hilly parkland and then the Greenford golf courses adjoined the canal. Posh sods cursing their kids and other halves whilst daydreaming of the young office totty and looking forward to a beer.

Soon afterwards the canal turned south into suburban Middlesex. I drifted through the industrial estates; the Paddington Arm soon reached the junction with the main line of the Grand Union Canal at Bull's Bridge. Cowley Lock marked the twenty-seven-mile run: nearly home. Not long now until the Colne Valley and Chiltern Hills. Uxbridge to the north; I'd woken up there a few times dazed, confused and hungover having fallen asleep on the train. London's claws were retracting. Uxbridge Lock had an attractive setting with its lock cottage. I wished more of England had retained its style. Too much had been destroyed and replaced by uglier, modern new builds. I stared at the turn-over bridge and beautiful, tall, modern flower mill standing nearby in grounds that were immaculately landscaped down to the water's edge. If I could have used both hands I would have applauded what I was appreciating.

Instead, I thanked whoever was responsible for redeeming a fraction of my faith in humanity. Perhaps in my madness I wouldn't feel obliged to press the fire button on the nuclear bombs just yet; ending it all for everyone and everything was a bit extreme.

I remembered the *Paddington Packet* mentioned in my guide book. It was a boat famous for doing the run daily from Paddington to Cowley, one of the few passenger boats that did that stretch of the Grand Union Canal. It was pulled by four horses and had precedence over all other boats so it was capable of covering the fifteen-mile lock-free run in a time that was remarkable at the beginning of the nineteenth century. I wondered who would have used it daily and whether they had felt the same about the journey as those stuffed on the jammed Metropolitan lines today, struggling to have enough room to even read their books or papers, fed up with sniffing other passengers' scents from long-digested meals of the night before.

The canal continued to meander northwards, gradually taking me closer to home. I passed the villages of Denham and across Harefield Moor. There, I slowed the boat, pulling up next to the reeds. This stretch of Common Land was of considerable interest to naturalists, and now me. I dropped the anchor and got Mason's bag out.

First I looked at his body. Most of the maggots had disappeared into his flesh although a few fell onto the floor of the boat. I would have liked to have just thrown him into the reeds, but I wasn't entirely convinced I could get him deep enough into the thicket and away from the water's edge for him to be invisible. I didn't want anything washing him into the water either, so I'd have to go in again and make sure he was well hidden out of sight. I didn't want to disturb the reeds too much as it was a site of interest and if it looked like someone had been wading around destroying the reeds that would soon be noticed. I could see some small runs, I guessed made by coots, moorhens or even a bittern or perhaps rats or desperate foxes. God knows, at least it was a way in.

I put the body back in the bag with the head – did I mention the two were separated? – and got undressed again, but this time I put my shoes back on. Getting on and off the boat would be a little easier due to the steps at the back of the boat, but stopping by the reeds was sure to raise suspicion, so I had to be as quick as possible and hope no one nosy came cruising by. At least the boat would provide some shelter once inside the water and on my way to the reeds.

I got in the freezing water again, which came up to my neck. With the body in the bag over my right shoulder, I waded until I reached the reeds' roots which gave a firmer footing. I was soon waist deep, and when I got to the small animal run I was crawling using my good elbow and legs and feet to push me on. Scrambling, I used every ounce of energy and physical strength I had left to get as deep into the reeds as possible. I had to close my eyes as putrid black swamp water burnt them and filled my nose with noxious gases whilst sharp reeds stabbed and scratched at my neck and face. I wriggled on until I felt like the reeds were closing in on me and I no longer had the strength to push any further into the reeds. I lay panting in the wet for a second.

The bag on my back felt so heavy and I felt stuck. I tried to turn one way to look behind me but couldn't move. I wanted to see if I could catch sight of the boat but I couldn't see behind me. It felt like someone was sitting on my back. I let go of the bag but it didn't move and I tried to pull my arm back in front of me but it was stuck behind me. I felt like I was trapped in a spider's web. I tried to move my wounded arm but it had no feeling at all. I was fucked: I had no strength left, the reeds had impaled me and I couldn't reverse. I felt tears in my eyes. I saw Chloe's face in my mind and relaxed. I closed my eyes.

2 – CASUAL

THE BOY IN FRONT OF ME looked into their faces, trying his best to not look scared. These lads were big, much bigger than the ones who'd whacked me in my last school. I'd learnt my lesson then; these kids were over a foot taller than me and had my entire attention.

'Mod or casual?' they sneered.

'Mod,' the little lad said, visibly shaking. I had to try to not look scared.

Whack: a punch in his guts for all his troubles and down he went in a snivelling, snotty-nosed bundle. Given the same choice I opted for the 'Casual' option. I stood as defiant as possible, trying not to laugh through my fear, knees feeling weak. I got away with a shove and was told, 'You don't look much like a casual!'

Sticks and stones may break my bones but words will never hurt me… unless they suggest I don't look right.

So the next weekend I returned from a shopping trip to Basildon with my mum with a new spiked haircut with a slightly long bit at the back (she got a perm) and I was kitted out in the latest imitation gear, or 'imo' as it was better known in Essex. I went for a Gino Capelli black, white and grey striped jumper, a pair of fairly tight drain-pipe jeans with little lines running through them and a shiny new pair of 'check me out I'm mega wicked cool' Nike Jammer trainers. I had never known love for shoes quite like it. Thanks to my mum I might not have been a proper casual but Bas Vegas didn't care: to Basildon, the land of the shellsuit, genuine gold-plated jewellery and family cars with go-faster stripes, I looked proper casual and mega wicked and a cool dude, especially if anyone ever bothered asking me again – and they could ask the bloke on the market stall who kitted me out if they didn't believe me.

I was nearly nine years old and fashion conscious.

3 – IS IT WRONG?

THANKFULLY MY FISHING CHAIR stopped my bum getting wet. I'm not sure that I would have felt it any way. Even my maggots were too cold to wriggle. My hands looked like red, bloated gloves, and even clapping them together and rubbing them and blowing on them seemed to help little, and it gave me a headache. Why was I here? The sun was bright and blinding to look at yet absent of any heat. I had woken up at four in the morning to sit here in the pissing cold trying to catch frigging fish and hadn't caught a flipping thing yet. I'd seen and heard the noisy green parrots flying through the trees; even these foreign invaders were more likely to catch a glimpse of the illusive barbel than me. It seemed funny seeing a parrot and yet never catching a native fish. Was that a racist thought? Perhaps they'd all swum off to warmer, exotic waters like the sparrows had.

Was it wrong to worry about being remembered when you were dead, buried and long gone? Was it a bit weird? I often worried no one would know I liked fishing or looking at pretty ladies or even what my favourite music was or where I had travelled and what I had seen.

I wondered if either of my granddads had liked fishing or looking at ladies. I guessed they both had to a certain extent, as I wouldn't have existed had they not had the inclination. I remembered fishing with both of them and I supposed fishing and looking at girls was quite similar in a strange sort of way. I wouldn't have wanted to snog a seven-pound chub mind, nor catch a fourteen-stone Geordie.

I could have sat there for hours and not caught a thing. I don't suppose anyone would get very far in life if they never saw anyone that caught their eye, and neither set of my grandparents would have ever met either.

When I died would people know who my friends were?

4 – KID WARFARE

I LOVED GROWING UP IN A HOUSE that backed onto woods. Directly behind our garden were two ponds full of newts, fish, frogs, dragonflies and monstrous tadpole-eating larvae and great diving beetles, pond skimmers and skaters, water boatman and every other weird creature little boys would love to keep as pets that sisters and mums just didn't and never would.

I guarded and loved those ponds and could quite easily have committed murder protecting them. One lad made the mistake of taking a bucketload of frogspawn and spilling some onto the gravel path as I watched. The thought of hundreds of little tadpoles dying, frying in the sun, was just too much for me and I saw red. My sister later heard through the school grapevine that I'd chucked Jimmy Taylor in the pond. You don't mess with the frogspawn on my watch. She said his dad was going to get me and I was in trouble. I was prepared to chuck the tadpole murderer's father in the pond as well. Those ponds were excellent.

The banks of the pond were also the scene for numerous, vicious clay wars, fought from either side. Two teams, we'd lob pieces of clay at each other; the only rule being 'no stones', unless you wrapped them in mud; that was my interpretation of the rules anyway. It was a bit like grenade fighting in trenches, minus the guns and uniforms.

We saw some odd sights there as well. I guess I was in one of the last generations of kids that were allowed to be kids and, to a certain extent, run wild –when summers lasted six weeks and were always hot, and the winters, snowy. It was before the media was filled with stories of child rapists, murderers and the like. In fact as a kid the first lesson I got on not talking to strangers was from a strange talking cat which somewhat ironically became massive on the rave scene when he and I got a little older.

One day, whilst playing by the ponds, my friends and I noticed a six-foot frog jump out of some bushes about fifty metres away and casually stroll off up a woodland path. At the time I was massively concerned about what it would eat as I'd not seen many three-foot worms on my travels and would be absolutely bricking it if I saw a fly big enough to satisfy a six-foot frog's appetite. It didn't occur to any of us that it was a strange man dressed in a costume creeping around the woods. We discussed firing a few arrows at it but didn't want it to chase us; a frog that big would be capable of leaping mega fast and over a massive distance for sure.

We would regularly search the streets and front gardens for newly planted shrubs and plants, ideally hunting those with the small green bamboo supports as these made the best arrows. We'd then select a nice branch, hack it from the tree, strip its bark, bend it and, using heavy duty fishing line, complete a bow. At a young age a few of us became very good at archery.

It wasn't only the ponds in the woods that my mates and I felt a collective protective responsibility towards; it was also a badger set – a fairly famous one, having been included in the Bayern Tapestry. We would often search for fresh tracks and signs of poachers.

On one occasion Minesh vanished from sight like in a magic trick Paul Daniels could only have dreamed of recreating. One minute a group of us were rummaging around and the next second whoosh, he vanished into thin air. We went to the hole nearest where he was standing last, absolutely flabbergasted. We looked all around the area. No one had ever vanished before our eyes and it felt terrible. It was well out of order, having a mega skill like that and not telling your friends first. We all started calling out for him whilst looking around the undergrowth, trees and branches, waiting for him to stroll out laughing, but nothing. He was right there then vamoose, gone.

Then we saw his hands scrambling in the depths of the darkness of the badgers' hole. It was a big dark hole, excavated into finest Essex clay, and he had slid right down and completely out of sight. His hands, arms, fingers, nails were clawing like a mole in a microwave. We watched them fighting the darkness, spellbound. He came tearing out from mother earth's depths like a geyser, half crying, half screaming. He went straight into full pelt and we had to leg it all the way to his house before he believed the badgers were no longer chasing him. He reckoned they were going for his ankles. I didn't understand why he didn't just vanish again using his special powers.

On another occasion during our regular reccies (which stood for reconnaissance missions) we heard other kids in our badger area. Like a bunch of juvenile chimpanzees, we sprang into action. We climbed our favourite conker tree that was used for every surveillance issue encountered in the nearby vicinity, but in this instance we were unable to get a better picture of the disturbance. We decided the best thing to do, as a way of a warning, would be to fire off a couple of arrows. We did this and nothing much happened. We fired off a couple more whilst the others, still in the tree, kept a look out. Still nothing; Minesh stayed in the tree, he was the best climber and newly appointed 'mega-skilful-dissapearer'. The twins joined me, Peter, Joe and Tony, and we all let loose a couple of arrows each.

The other kids went quiet. Good, we thought, they must have got the message and decided to sneak away, cluck, cluck chickens!

'What's going on Minesh?' I whisper-hissed.

'Nothing,' he said.

'Where are they?' I said, still whisper-hissing.

'Don't know, I can't see them,' Minesh said.

Then we heard them, like faint whistles or rockets in the woods, leaves being torn and then cracks of tree trunks. Dirty tactics, I decided, throwing stones; probably not even covered in clay. Well out of order. We shot the rest of our arrows in their direction and waited again. More whistles, like fireworks on Guy Fawkes' Night, only much quieter. More cracking on bark, lots of whistles now.

'Flipping hell,' I screamed, looking up into the trees. They were being aimed into the trees near Minesh. 'Minesh, what's going on?'

'Big!' Minesh squawked.

'Big what, Minesh? You flipping Joey!' I asked, sensing the panic rising.

'Big kids coming!'

We glanced up to the brow of the hill and to our horror there were at least twelve big kids running straight for us. I looked up as Minesh grabbed a weak branch and it cracked, lowering him a full building's height a little faster than comfortable and back into our group. I couldn't believe it, the well lucky git; he should have at least sprained his ankle or broken his leg or chipped a tooth. We all broke out into a mad dash, proper pegging it for our lives, as more missiles rattled all around us.

'I think they've got guns,' I shouted as we hurdled down through the bracken, every shortcut utilised, back to the ponds and alongside my house's back garden and finally the leap from the broken tree trunk and over the fence and into my space. We all bolted like a pack of trapeze artists and sat puffing and panting, searching the fence for signs that our pursuers were going to follow us into my garden. But they didn't; we had lost them.

Minesh pulled out a metal ball bearing and said it was what the big boys had been firing at us. The twins said they were adventure scouts and they had a cousin who was one; they were all well hard and proper skitzos so we were well lucky. *Next time we should use sharper arrows*, I thought. Those black widow catapults with ball bearings were a powerful adversary to any group of kids.

5 – GOSH

MY EARLIEST MEMORIES were as a boy in hospital in London. I remember watching my piss go up tubes. Big black mamas came along and washed me by picking me up by the ankles and roughly going over my privates with a wet flannel. I wondered if they used the same flannel on all the kids. I wondered if they were actually nurses or just people who took advantage of sick kids whilst nobody noticed.

I remembered coming round after being in theatre and, although drowsy, convinced I still had the strength to play with the other children. I jumped down from my bed and landed in a heap from the waist down. I still had no feeling.

I sometimes wondered if memories like this, the being fairly fucked, vulnerable, a bit out of it, were half the reason in subsequent years I sought to replicate my earliest memories.

One particular night in bed on the ward sticks in my mind. Strange kids lay in different beds all around me, all of them ill to a different extent. It was dark, clinical and morbid. Some kids were beyond much help. To me it was all irrelevant, and I didn't want to be there as much as any other kid, but this was what had been deemed necessary and the best course of action for a better later life. Kids, though, don't know, never know, how lives can be made better or worse. Words of encouragement and understanding only last as long as the sentence in which they are uttered. Kids just want to play, be at home, with toys and friends or cuddling Mummy and Daddy or Flopsy the rabbit. They don't want to feel trapped, lonely, violated, imprisoned in a hospital. Scared, scared even of the other sick kids that cry at night. Kids don't understand that other kids have the same fears.

That's when I saw the white ghost drifting down the corridors, walking alongside the wards, looking through the windows in search of her baby. I was the baby.

'Here I am, Mummy.'

She had come to rescue me and take me home; she looked at me in my bed and stopped. Why didn't she come in? But she couldn't come in. She wasn't allowed, but I didn't know that. One hand on the glass partition was all that separated us. Half a wave, half a gentle motherly caress, and then she was gone and I was alone and the ward fell silent again. The ghost had gone, my ghost had gone. All that was left were the muffled sounds of kids alone with their pain.

I remembered being wheeled to the lift on the way to theatre. A few lungfuls of gas and I was off into dream land. If I had known how bad it would be when I woke up, like most kids I wouldn't have been half as worried about the whole going to sleep bit. I still maintained, though, that all operations on children should be done in the middle of the night. That would be understandable to a kid. Lots of strange things happen in the night. It's when crazy big red blokes come down your chimney, it's when monsters come out from under your bed, tooth fairies dish out the money for your well-wiggled teeth, the world transforms into a winter wonderland. It's when you wake up and the whole world has suddenly changed. It's normal to go to sleep and when you wake up things are different. It's wrong to go to bed, wake up, be wide awake, get told to be brave and then get put back to sleep whilst alert and fully aware of all the bad stuff that's going on around you. Bad things happen when you go to sleep in the middle of the day.

6 – PILOT LIGHT

I HARDLY EVEN BOTHERED telling my colleagues I was going to lunch any more. I flicked my name out on a board indicating whether I was in or out of the office and slunk away.

I'd often just walk up and down Chapel Market, desperate for someone to talk to outside my office. Just a bit of normality is what I craved; I started smiling as soon as I left the building. I stopped at Bryan's rice and pea stall to buy some jerk chicken. If he asked how I was he'd find me busily struggling to justify my own existence. In my imaginary conversations with him I normally got it sorted, so by the time I was at the front of the queue and ready to order in the end I just had the same conversation we usually had, which ended on me saying, 'Have a good day, mate.'

So I'd go back to work, sit at my desk and eat my lunch. Trying to ignore the ringing phones, I would carry on my conversation with Bryan in my head, now determined to explain myself.

I was known as Pilot Light, supposedly because I never went out. It was an old-school, supposed requisite of the job, apparently, to go out and do boozy lunches. I worked in the print industry. My general job title would be account director, manager, sales rep or handler depending on who you spoke to in the company. The role included finding and keeping happy people who produce printed items, and then wining and dining them as often as proved necessary in order to ensure they used my company to produce as much as possible of their printed items. It was presumed, by my esteemed established colleagues, that bribery was the only way to ensure work. I had always been of the inclination that my job and role were better served within the company by my always being available to cater for my client's needs: reactive more than proactive.

I never liked or wanted to be a pushy salesman. Whether I was preparing a quick quote or answering whether a job was possible (within certain time restraints) or even supplying samples of previous projects, if I was out getting pissed, I wasn't likely to be capable of doing both. This led to the nickname Pilot Light. Because I never went out, it was presumed I was doing something wrong. I was mocked, but I believed I knew my clients and what they wanted from me better than my peers – but who knows for sure. I liked to think they understood my thinking better when they started struggling to get reimbursed for their work expenses. But that was all they worked for. Every day going out and getting pissed for a living! It was a dodgy job and one that led to more than one person I knew losing the plot on drink and drugs. I didn't really believe it was necessary and felt sorry for the ones who couldn't see they were addicted.

If you're lucky you can find like-minded people who enjoy your company as well as use your company. What your colleagues and clients might never know is what you get up to when you go out. The work you and the real you don't always meet. I'd always thought shitting on your own doorstep was best avoided. So knowing what I was like when I went out was possibly asking a little too much. Sometimes things are best left to the imagination of others. I always figured my clients knew me well enough to imagine what I'd be like to go out with regularly and were quite happy not to do it more than necessary for fear of damaging both of our mental well-beings.

7 – AFTER DARK

DAD WOULD COME AND WAKE ME in the middle of the night. I'd put on a woolly hat and pick up my torch and off we'd go into the darkness. Dad's torch was a proper, standard man's type, no flair, durable, waterproof, heavy, two settings, full beam and half, bright and direct, lighting fifty metres of night-time woodland track. My torch, in comparison, was silver with a red plastic head, light and fairly weak, but had various buttons that, once utilised, changed the light to different colours: red, blue, green and the standard. We'd walk through the woods.

Most people would think we were mad, or Dad at least was mad. I wasn't scared, though; I was with my Dad. Actually, I was sometimes, like if we heard something crashing through the undergrowth. One time we walked into a family of badgers busily scoffing, grunting and running around. They didn't seem to care that we were there. I suppose the fact that we stood dead still, transfixed, gate-crashing their night-time forays, meant they could just get on with whatever they were doing. Another time we stumbled across some poachers, hunting for rabbits. I think they were more scared of us emerging from the darkness. I expect they thought we could have been park rangers or the police, but once they knew it was a bloke and his son they relaxed. They introduced me to the Jack Russell that was excited about going down holes to search for its quarry. They were quite open and friendly people, just looking for some food. Another time we found a glow-worm on a path on a particularly starry night. We lay down for a while looking at the stars as bats skimmed over us, shooting out sonar squeaks as they hunted bugs, and the moon was so bright we didn't need our torches to see where we were going.

It was heaven as a kid growing up there. A magpie turned up on our street one day: it was as mad as a hat, it tried to peck my sister's toes. It was as friendly as you like, too friendly really. All the neighbours had to shut their windows to stop it coming in their houses, worried it would nick their jewellery. As soon as you went outside it would swoop down and try to land on your head or shoulders. I thought it was great and would have loved to have kept it as a pet. It even made a big dog run away, chattering like a rattle – I thought it was laughing. Unfortunately someone came and took it away. One day someone brought a squirrel into school but it was well mad as well and some girls screamed and didn't like it either so it wasn't allowed in again. Another day a dog ran around the school playground and we chased him for ages, and another time a great black-backed gull poohed on one of the other little boy's backs. It was great; it went all the way from his head down to his bum. The dinner lady told me off for laughing at him because he had to wear his PE kit all day.

8 – RECESSION

I WAS RUNNING ACROSS CROXLEY GREEN thinking about the last conversation I'd had with Chloe's dad. I'd tried to explain it all to him: how I saw it all panning out. He'd tried to understand. I was running and hadn't planned a route. I'd put on my trainers and shorts and top and run out the door. I was being carried along by my iPod's random selections. Some songs made me run on with a steely determination, others made me want to stop and weep. Where I was running to and what was I running from I hadn't decided. I felt like I was in training for something and hadn't yet learnt what it was. I was knackered; perhaps now would be a good time to head home, I thought. I found myself explaining myself to myself. Nobody was interested, nobody cared.

When the inevitable recession had hit, the last sector that was properly screwed was the financial market. Those that worked in marketing or in retail, in travel industry or those in print like me had felt the effects for ages and known it was coming. We had long since tightened our belts before the rich City boys felt the pinch. First the marketing budgets were cut; that meant overstaffed creative agencies shed excess staff. Then it started becoming difficult to find work. Different people started purchasing what little print was being produced from preferred suppliers or, worse still, the cheapest print companies; in turn printers battled each other by lowering costs, and the weakest companies folded.

Although this was happening for years whilst fat cat bankers continued paying themselves massive bonuses, eventually even the financial market stopped producing so much print, instead opting to send group emails rather than printing monthly reports. Design and media agencies still pitched for new business, architects still produced plans, books were still being sold. Life went on, it was just increasingly difficult.

I had to find different markets to my preferred financial sector. I became hardened to hearing about other people's hard times. I knew about the recession years before it affected most people; most people understood, though. The ones who had to battle to survive were the ones who paid for the fat cats to get their bonuses for causing the problem in the first place.

In a dog-eat-dog world everyone is a potential meal, even if you're a vegetarian.

I thought I had a blister.

9 – ESSEX EXPRESS

AS MY MUM SET ABOUT HER WEEKLY SHOP, Dad would mooch off and check out the hi-fi or running magazines or latest electrical items for sale in the new one-stop-mega-shop that was Sava Centre in Bas Vegas. I soon got bored of checking out which Transformer had the most strength and speed and could only bounce the plastic footballs back into their metal housing for so long before a miserable shelf stacker or an old lady with a tartan push trolley would start moaning, so off I wandered. Little boys copy their fathers.

At the entrance to the shop was a crazy water feature with a giant clockwork mechanism that to any engineer like my father was a thing of moving, metal wonder. I just saw a massive money pit. I learnt quickly it was okay to take the money out if it looked like you were throwing it back in. Disapproving stares soon turned to blind eyes: I was basically recycling other people's wishes. I was young and didn't know any better. I was someone else's problem child.

I enjoyed skimming the two pence pieces, especially if I managed to get them into the eternal workings of the machine. I was always hopeful of causing carnage to the moving parts. Also, if you got the angle correct you could skim from one pool into the other as surrounding the massive clock were compartmented, separate water wells. It was whilst skimming from section to section that I'd occasionally strike it rich and be able to grab a silver coin. These beauties wouldn't be thrown back; these found their way into Martin the Newsagent's tills and gifted me Panini football stickers. I never did manage to get the Meadowbank Thistle gold badge. I always seemed to need, need, need, need, need whereas the other kids just got, got, got and needed to complete. I'd also purchase a Lemonade Sparkle ice lolly which would need to be consumed double quick before meeting back up with Mum and Dad and my suspicious sisters. They always seemed to sense when I'd had something they hadn't.

I realised I was getting out of my depth when, guilt-ridden, I admitted my crimes to a priest during confession and then gave my pocket money to the clockwork fountain as a way of saying sorry and doing my penance. This wasn't until I'd discovered my scam and crime of the century: 'the grand cake theft'. I'd learnt that I could go to the cake counter and order two iced fingers and two doughnuts without needing to pay a penny, and then calmly walk to the rear of the shop where upstairs they had a buffet-style cafe with toilets. Here I'd find myself a free cubicle where I'd stuff my face before ripping up the box and flushing it down the loo. It was the perfect crime. I was always a fussy eater as a kid, but at times I really wasn't hungry much, to the utter frustration of my parents. I left some money on the cake counter in the hope that in some way it repaid my debt to society.

My adventures got further afield as I learnt to gauge exactly how long a 'big shop' took when compared to one of Mum's 'quick grabs'. 'Big shop' soon meant I could get as far as the arcades in Eastgate. I could check out the Chinese karate shop and look longingly at the numbchucks, punching mitts and ninja stars and other fighting tools. Other times I'd just mess about in my sister's favourite shop, Confetti, with the glittery silver and gold pens. Although undoubtedly a girly shop that sold all types of pens, diaries and pads and papers, and all sorts of things to ignore, I'd still take my time writing a few rude words and my name 'woz ere' and 'West Ham United rule' before running off to the old market on the other side of the town centre behind the strange water fountain with a massive, wet, bronze lady lying down with a baby. Although that mission proved more of a 'leggit' run and didn't leave anywhere near enough time to talk with the swearing parrot in the smelly pet shop or look at the farting powder or other funny tricks in the joke shop.

Occasionally my wanderings as a lad became infectious and as a group my friends and I would set off on our bikes. We called it scrambling. Some days we were the BMX Bandits, others the Red Hang Gang if everyone had something red on. If anyone wanted to be the A-Team I always wanted to be Face, but put up with being Murdock. Minesh was always BA.

Every day was an adventure. We soon knew hundreds of routes all around the woods that backed onto my house. Some routes climbed steadily uphill past the conker tree lookout post until they came out at the Crown pub, sitting proudly at the top of the hill looking out over the bad lands of Bas Vegas, past Langdon Hills and Laindon, all the way to the other side of the world. Another route passed Frog Alley, where we'd seen the giant frog, alongside the two ponds, and would come out on the far side of my school. Another route brought you out near the 'rec' (short for recreational ground, or swings and slides). No land was left unchartered, no empty, abandoned house (due for demolition) left unsearched for forgotten treasure. The empty houses were being knocked down for the new housing developments or more roads that were eating away at the little pockets of countryside I knew around the area called home.

On one scrambling mission to the pits (which were old bomb craters in the woods where the German Nazis had dropped their bombs before heading home), I learnt the importance of proper bike maintenance. Something about being a lad meant everything, no matter how much I treasured it, needed testing to the limit – and in most cases, destruction – even my favourite belongings. This time it was my trusty steed, my bicycle; it was by far my most valued item in the world. Everything, I knew, was possible on my bike, and although it wasn't a mongoose or diamond-back like all the spoilt, rich kids craved, it was a proper BMX and it did have bright yellow plastic mags spokes and equally sunny matching mushroom handlebar grips. It was in fact a bright yellow and red beast, armed with a padded front handlebar for your head and padded nut bar to protect your balls should you fall off your seat. That was, at least, until I burst the rear tyre after doing multiple skids. To make it even better Dad replaced the old rear tyre with a blue one, mental. I had a yellow, red and blue bike and it was well wicked.

I was mega wicked at pretty much all the tricks: endos, bunny hops, no handers. All unfortunately and sometimes painfully learnt by trial and error, meaning that although my bike was sturdy it had certainly been put through the mill. One problem arose from my over-eager skidding practice... On this particular scrambling mission my front brake had already given up the ghost and I had to tie the loose cable around the frame of the bike. I didn't have the Cubs badge for knots, although I was quite capable of producing sufficient fishing and reef variations and several styles of shoelace bows. It wasn't much of a problem as in most of my scrambling missions tearing down woody hills, jumping roots and doing skids required little front brake action due to not wanting to perform front wheel skids or any impromptu, unnecessary flights over the handlebars. But as I hurtled down the wooded tracks, arms vibrating like a worker on a pneumatic drill, my back brake snapped, leaving me with no brakes at all. My only options were to try to sit down and use my feet (not an option at that speed), or try to stay on as long as possible like a bucking bronco, or dive off the bike entirely.

I tore down the hill past my friends, leaving them amazed at my sudden, all-out, no-fear approach. They tried to keep up, peddling like crazy. The path went one way and I went another down the side of a hill. Like a Ewok on a speeda bike I flew past trees. They became bigger and closer. I struggled to avoid more and more bushes and shrubbery as the thicket became denser and denser. My face was getting scratched by brambles.

Finally my bike was enveloped by a thick bush and I was flung through the air, deep into the foliage. I lay still, battered and bruised, until my mates hacked their way into the vegetation to find me in my winded, wounded state. Once sitting up, I sneaked a quick look at my willy; the handlebars had twisted and on impact caught me straight on the dude, and amazingly I had a bruise to prove it. I let the other lads wheel my bashed-up bike back to my house as they each relayed stories of how 'well wicked' my stack was; it was the stuff of legends and I was a hero. I wouldn't show them my bruise, though; just talking about it made them grab their nuts and roll around the floor in sympathetic agony.

10 – IT STARTED

IT STARTED IN A SIMILAR FASHION to when I'd felt like I was losing everything before – an escalation in situations that if they had occurred at a single time would have been easy to cope with, but unfortunately these things happened like dominoes, one after another, all of them piling pressure on an already maxed-out hard drive: my head.

It was gone ten at night and I was still at work, tired, just sitting staring at the computer screen. I couldn't be bothered to start the trek home in the cold. I was hungry but couldn't be bothered to eat. I had to finish my invoicing, depressing as it was. I'd put it off almost all month in the hope that a large job might come in to rescue another shitty month. What was the point in getting commission if you couldn't even beat your targets? I guessed lions didn't have targets to meet: one antelope and that was food for the pride for a few days. I supposed a drought was like a recession. Where was my pride?

Emotion is one sense the brain seems to struggle to control. Allegedly, it is what separates us from the animals: the more highly tuned we have become, so our caring capabilities have become stronger or weaker. I wasn't sure any more. Nearly all animals care for their young to some extent, whether protecting or setting up a nice house or laying down their lives shielding their offspring. Some care for others' young as well, making crèches. It's even been known occasionally for animals to adopt other breeds of animals like lions and gazelles or elephants and dogs or owls and pussy cats, and in some cases some animals become friends.

Humans, however, are judged in an almost opposite, different fashion. It's more about how kind you are; this somehow reflects the more human you are. The less emotion you show, the less human you seem. We are intrigued by animals that do the things we like humans to do; somehow it makes them seem more human, kind even. So it seems an insult to animals to describe a bad person as an animal.

11 – OUR SOUL TRAIN

ON OUR WAY INTO SCHOOL we would push ourselves up against the windows on the single carriage trains to make it seem like the compartment was full. Normally there would be me, James, Roy, Liam, Greeney and Mason and maybe a few others. Sometimes we'd swing the heavy wooden doors open just as we were entering the station so anyone standing too close to the edge of the platform would need to dive back to avoid being knocked to kingdom come. We stopped doing this around the time our teacher actually got hit by a door and spent some time in hospital with multiple broken bones; he looked like he'd been beaten up by Mike Tyson.

On one journey we removed the light bulbs and threw them on the M25 as the train passed overhead. We created a dust storm Egypt would have been proud of by bashing the seats until everyone found breathing difficult; all our clothes, hair and hands covered in dust or, as we called it, 'dead man's skin'. We then removed the seats to check for money and climbed up and sat on the baggage rails; not that it was more comfortable or anything, it was just different to sitting on the seats like normal humans.

For some reason Mason decided a little prematurely to open the train door, thinking we were coming into Shenfield. Sometimes we would slide open the window and lean out, getting 'Chinese eyes'; it was like putting your face in an industrial-strength blower. We didn't do it much after hearing stories of a boy's head coming off after being hit by another train. The old style trains had a stiff sliding latch I dreaded for years as a kid; the thought of not being able to open the door and being stuck on the train – God only knows where I'd end up, I presumed Scotland. Whatever happened I'd probably die if I didn't get off the train.

Mason, the ginger kid who could get into a fight in an empty room, pushed open the door with no trouble at all. He got it far too early, though. I reckoned because we had no lights and the compartment was so dusty he figured we were nearer than we really were; either that or he needed some fresh air. The door was open and he stepped down onto the standing board step. It was only then that I noticed him properly, as he balanced precariously. I remember him looking round at us; although not a best friend, still that look of a fellow traveller and conspirator was etched onto his face. The face of a fellow train wrecker.

Then he slipped, falling through the air. We lurched forward collectively, trying to grab him before he fell, but we were too late. We saw him fall. Terror in his pale, freckled face. His ginger head hit the floor first and his scalp was ripped away. Blood spurted everywhere as his eye was snatched clean out of his head. Arms and legs snapped on impact, and as the momentum carried him along bits of his body were torn clean off, leaving only his torso encased in his tattered school blazer with the school badge sitting proud.

All of us knew the cops would think we'd killed him and our parents would probably ground us. That was not good as we had the Saint Helen's school disco coming up and Mandy Parker and her mates were likely to be there and some of them were well sexy and would let you touch them up and everything.

That didn't happen. The moment the door opened and we realised we were nowhere near the platform and the group of us instinctively knew this could be dangerous, as Mason slipped we all lurched forward to grab him. Greeney caught his arm first. This caused some concern as Greeney as Mason had never been that friendly and had only recently been squabbling with him to the point of fisticuffs. Mason was leaning back like a limbo dancer, bag dangling precariously, getting buffeted by the train's movements and the wind from the cool, damp, dark night. His outstretched arm was held by Greeney who in turn was sliding through the door being held by Liam; Liam who in turn wasn't that keen on either Mason or Greeney. James and I grabbed Liam and for a few moments everyone considered Greeney considering whether to let go. Thankfully we all pulled each other back into the carriage as we arrived at Shenfield station platform. It was mentioned that Greeney had saved Mason's life, a fact neither of them seemed too happy about. I was just relieved that I wasn't going to get grounded and still had a chance of a snog with Mandy at the Saint Helen's disco.

12 – JAMES

I'D TOLD JAMES before it wasn't really in our plans, but he was adamant that I should keep the pressure on Chloe and that babies were the way forward and I'd be a great dad.

We were catching up over a few beers and something to eat. We were in one of those modern country pubs that could be a chain; it had a warm, stuffy, stifling ambiance, no music, no air and people who talked too loudly about nothing and James talked louder still until I couldn't take it any more, fidgeting in my seat, trying to stop my eyes rolling and my brain switching off. I was gasping for some air. I wanted to change the subject. My eyes were dry and I couldn't help yawning. I looked around, searching for an escape route.

His Catholic family upbringing had sent his parental ethos into overdrive, and if it transpired that he and everyone else had messed up their lives by having kids then so should I. Why did I always start arguments in my head as a way of distracting myself from the actual topic? Why didn't I just tell James to back off? Perhaps he was right and I was scared of the truth. Life was a struggle for sure, but he seemed happy enough. He loved his boy unquestionably. Everybody I knew who had kids loved them unequivocally. What if Chloe and I were different? What if we had kids we didn't love? Would our friends and family still support us, or would they say it was our fault, our decision to have kids, our responsibility... could we turn around and say 'You said we should have kids, that we would be good parents, but you're wrong, we're bad parents, I hate my child'?

All of what he said sounded great, although a bit sound-bitey. I'd heard it all a thousand times before. Everyone kept saying: meet a girl, fall in love, get married, settle down, have kids. It was all so easy, so premeditated. I had no idea if I'd be a good dad. I certainly liked the idea, although it also frightened me, and although it had always been Chloe who was more against the idea than me, I sort of felt like I didn't deserve it either. I wanted to be with Chloe and wanted to be with her no matter what, even if that meant no kids.

At the turn of the millennium I had been deep in a messy relationship. Although we had been together for several years there were always trust issues anyway. Somehow we'd had the opportunity to have a child, but the decision had been taken away from me. My girlfriend at the time had discovered she was pregnant. She was unsure of what to do, and although my family offered support to the point of actually saying they'd support me and the child if it came to it, the decision was taken away by the girlfriend's parents who booked her in to have an abortion before my girlfriend's feet had touched the ground and we had had a proper chance to weigh up the situation. I was treated like a naughty schoolchild and cut out of the loop. I didn't have a great job but I was working. I could have coped, but in the end it wasn't to be and any chance of finding out was snatched away.

So I bitterly said to James, 'Look, mate, I've had my chance, it was taken away, you know when, and besides, it might not have even been my child and I still can't get that out of my head. Fuck it, Chloe and I are too selfish. She wants lots of holidays and money and freedom. She has a good job even if I'm struggling with mine. If I want to share these things with her I can't afford babies!'

James conceded and backed down, I think for the first time in our lives.

13 – REDDEN COURT

I HAD MISSED THE LAST COACH FROM SCHOOL to Harold Wood. It wasn't exactly a pleasant walk; in actual fact for a young lad it was a little daunting – a few miles taking in the wonders of Havering and Essex's finest alongside the A127. I knew some back alleys and shortcuts, but for a short twelve-year-old with a rucksack full of text books and rugby kit and one hand carrying a clarinet box, I must have resembled a bully's textbook victim: a tortoise with a musical instrument. Plus, rumours were rife about fights with the school next door, Redden Court. They didn't like the Campion Gay boys, as we were known, and the red badge acted like a target on my blazer from at least one hundred metres.

I walked as fast as my legs would get me to the station. Unfortunately, though, I wasn't nearly fast enough. The first broken brick landed not far to the right of me in a puff of exploding concrete, the second just behind me, sending shivers down my spine. I glanced back to see big lads running fast, hurdling bushes, scrambling around the corner towards me. *Leg it*, I thought, as the adrenalin breathed life into my temporarily terrified, frozen body. I stopped myself wanting to curl up into a ball like a hedgehog. All too quickly I could hear heavy feet rapidly gaining on me with every step I made.

The first youth sped up to me. 'Run, for fuck's sake,' he said.

I was running, I couldn't run much faster. I could hear shouting and jeering.

'Come on then, you fucking wankers.'

More footsteps catching me up just as quickly then whoosh, in a running blur my clarinet box was snatched from my hand as a big kid raced past. More flying rubble, more shouting and goading, even louder and faster footsteps closing in behind me.

'Oi, give me back my flipping clarinet,' I shouted at the big kid who'd run on in front of me. But it was no good; he wasn't stopping. More big kids ran past me then wallop, my rucksack was pulled off my shoulder, spinning me round. What the hell was going on? One more lad was coming up behind me, the biggest of the lot, so big he almost blocked out the world as he bore down on me. At the last moment when I expected him to crush me like a steam roller I could see behind him the source of the flying rocks and abuse: it was Redden Court! I turned to start running again, trying to catch up with my bag and clarinet.

'Run, you idiot,' the big lad said.

'I am running!' I shouted back. I was one of the fastest in my year in long distance, but I was rubbish at sprinting: my arms were pumping like Daley Thompson but my legs were going in slow motion.

'Don't make me carry you!' the big lad said.

'I don't wanna be carried,' I shouted back.

The chasing mob was getting closer and closer but he wasn't leaving me behind. We legged it all the way to the station, two roads under continual bombardment. As we ran up the hill to the station we could see a train was approaching. The rocks and shouting kept coming, my legs and heart and lungs were burning. We ran into the station and were chased down the stairs. We sprinted down to the end of the platform and crossed the tracks in front of the oncoming train. We ran back up the track on the opposite side, so we now had a train and a platform between us. The other big lads from my school were waiting at the doors of the train to pull us on and stop any of the pursuers. I was finally reunited with my clarinet and rucksack.

I had no excuse not to do my homework now, but at least I had some big new mates who all appreciated my crisps and taught me how to smoke.

14 – THE OFFICE

'UPSTAIRS IN THE BOARDROOM, five minutes, gloves off.'

The director's phone call was blunt. I knew I was due a bollocking over my shrinking sales figures, but the recession had hit everyone and this wasn't the way the financial director would deal with that situation; nope, that was still on the cards. This was about something else – what else had I done that could have pissed him off more than normal? I hadn't used my phone any more than usual, and I hadn't been looking at the internet more than usual either. Perhaps someone had got caught doing drugs and had blamed me? Not likely. I hadn't nicked anything, and I hadn't printed any KDs lately ('keep darks', as in keep them out of view of whoever you don't want to know you've printed something); well, I hadn't printed anything excessive bar perhaps my wedding stationery, photos and thank-you cards and both my sister and my brother-in-law's new business stationery – but apart from that, nothing major recently.

I went into the boardroom and didn't sit down. If I was going to be bollocked I wanted to know what for before I sat down and accepted it. Chris huffed in.

'Shut the door,' he half shouted. 'What the fuck did I ask you?' he continued.

'I don't know what you're talking about,' I replied, which was the truth, I really didn't. This was how I was when confronted with a question: if I hadn't already thought of an answer or got one planned, I wasn't likely to magic one out of thin air unless prompted.

'I'll tell you, shall I?'

Chris's voice was getting higher and all Balkan on me, which he is as well.

That would be nice, I thought. 'Okay,' I said instead.

'Don't say a fucking thing to Stan. Didn't I, didn't I?'

I now understood what the matter was. I'd had the pleasure of working with a bloke pretty much hated by everyone who worked with him, including most of the customers as well; most importantly, I supposed. His colleagues wanted him out, the management wanted an excuse, certain people were looking for a reason to stitch him up, and being a bunch of two-faced, lying, back-stabbing jobsworths counting the days until they retired they were all acting as slippery as snakes covered in Vaseline and decided to choose one of my clients to blame for a complaint made about the bloke everyone wanted rid of. I suppose it was the same office politics that happen everywhere, but right now it was happening to me and I didn't want any part of it.

Unfortunately when Chris told me he had heard from X that Y had said that Z wasn't giving us work any more because of 'the-bloke-that-everyone-hated-but-were-too-spineless-to-sack', I phoned my client and asked him directly for the truth. Two things struck me as odd. Firstly he was on holiday when the accusation was made, and secondly he wasn't the type of person to say that sort of thing, and when I asked him he said the same thing. He had no issues with the-lanky-bastard-that-everyone-hates.

On the morning when it all kicked off the-lanky-bastard-that-no-one-liked said to me, 'What's all this I'm hearing about Kevin not liking me and not giving us business any more because of me?'

'No idea, he's not said anything to me,' I said, which was all true. Following that discussion the-lanky-bastard-that-no-one-liked spoke to the other skinny bastard, the director (the guy now shouting at me), saying, 'I've spoken to Pilot Light and he said Kevin hasn't got a problem with me.' This wasn't what I said either, but the skinny bastard director had called the meeting and the gloves were now off.

'Why couldn't you just say, yes, Kevin complained or... or... or you didn't want to speak about it?'

I could see the blood pressure rising in the director's face. The veins in his neck looked like they were ready to burst, and his blinking eyes flicked between a rabbit in the headlights and a complete mentalist as he loomed over me.

'Because that's a lie,' I said.

'You made me look like a right fucking cunt,' said the director.

You did a fine job of that yourself, I thought. 'That's fucking bollocks, Chris,' I said. 'You're asking me to lie, and as much as I hate the lanky-bastard-that-everyone-hates my client didn't say what he's accused of saying – all this is bollocks. You're using me and my client as scapegoats. This has come round because other senior members of staff have got their knickers in a fucking twist and have been pulling your poxy chain. If you want to blame someone, blame one of those spineless fucks that actually did forward you customers' complaints, but don't have a go at me for not lying for you!'

I went back to my desk. I could feel my eye twitching and had that feeling when your heart is pounding and your head aches. I'd had a stupid row in the morning with Chloe, God knows what about, I think it might have been because I mentioned I wasn't keen on her fur coat and that somehow had sparked an almighty row. She was particularly prickly at the moment and I felt like every time I opened my mouth I was saying the wrong thing. I checked my mobile phone and saw I had a missed call from Dad and a snotty text message from Chloe. I deleted the message from Chloe accusing me of being nasty and evil and phoned my dad. Something was wrong with Grandad.

15 – RAT RACE

IT'S PROBABLY FAIR TO SAY I was a little bit goofy as a kid, and not just mentally. My mum always denied it, saying, 'You have big teeth. Sooner or later you'll grow into them, sweetheart.'

I didn't have a clue what she meant. I guess it was nicer than pointing out I could easily eat an apple through a tennis racket.

Like most kids I was forced into having several teeth removed so I could be fitted with a brace: the joys of puking up blood and going into school with a sausage tongue and amazing my mates with my jaws' newfound resilience which after a few punches gave way to a dull constant ache. No wonder babies cry when they're teething. I had a sharp, scaffolding train track fixed on the bottom and a removable, squashed-prawn plate on the top. I hated it, although I did manage to learn it was possible to turn the plate completely around in my mouth, which must have been pleasant viewing for the school teachers and my parents who would witness such mouth dexterity – still, it was the best way to get through the boredom of double geography lessons.

I also discovered problems, eating bacon for starters. Mum was keen on streaky bacon, but unfortunately, due to the long, fatty nature of its composition, unless it was crispy or cut into little nibbly bits, it could, if you were unlucky like me, get stuck to your brace.

Mum noticed me gagging and swallowing with eyes watering.

'What's wrong sweetheart, are you choking?' she said, hitting my back. I continued desperately chewing, trying to make a bite count, looking for a cutting edge on the meat, still with my eyes watering, gagging; I must have looked like a cat with a fur ball in its mouth.

'Brace!' I said like an evil alien. 'Can't swallow!'

Mum dived in fingers first, fishing around in my metal-filled mouth. She found the rasher stuck at the back of my gullet and then started tugging. Now my eyes were streaming, still gulping and gagging as I regurgitated. My sisters sat staring, mouths wide open, transfixed as the rasher went on and on, it was at least a foot long! I decided to lay off the bacon for about three years.

I was also lucky enough to be given a head brace that was supposed to be worn from the moment I got in from school till just before I left again in the morning. I tried to oblige, even though I could tell I was being laughed at, even by my mum and dad and my sisters, even the cat. But the final straw came when friends turned up to see if I was hanging out. Yeah, let's all laugh at the freak. I think neighbours even came round asking to borrow some sugar just to see if they could catch a glimpse of me.

It was like an old-fashion rugby hat, blue straps with silver latches or buttons on the side that connected via elastic bands that attached to a whisker-like piece of metal that went into my mouth and fitted neatly into a special connection on the brace.

I reckoned if I wasn't prepared to do the recommended hours I could cheat by upping the amount of elastic bands and only wear the damn thing when I went to bed. The elastic bands were the force that moved the teeth: no pain, no gain. You were supposed to have two on each side, but I became addicted to pain and elastic and soon was on four on each whisker. The next day I'd have to put up with self-induced headaches and a sore jaw, but it had to be better than looking like a mentalist or someone who'd had their head run over.

One night I decided to go for five bands on each side. I woke up in the middle of the night; I could hear a strange creaking in my head. I sat up in bed, looking around my room, my sleep-crusty eyes scanning, checking the dark: nothing to be seen. Still the strange creaking continued in my head, then I heard a crack and my brace came alive, attacking me like an angry crab, turning my head into a catapult and firing one of the buckles on the side of my head across the room like a bullet. The metal whiskers also came to life and one side pulled my brace out of the roof of my mouth and back towards my throat, gagging me. The buckle latch that was shot from the side of my head whistled through the air, hitting the furthest bedroom wall, and then rebounded, flying back to hit the wall behind me like a bullet in an old Yosemite Sam cartoon, ricocheting in front and behind me and then finally coming to a rest on my lap. I stuck my fingers in my mouth to stop myself getting an accidental Chelsea smile, then I sat in my bed, flummoxed. My goofy plans would perhaps take a little longer than anticipated.

16 – IT HAPPENED

NEXT STOP WAS BASILDON. I hadn't been there much since I was a kid. I was going to see my Grandad in hospital. I didn't know how long he'd be in there; I wasn't really sure what was wrong with him – he was never ill. I looked out of the window as the countryside raced by in a green and yellow blur, unsure what I could tell Grandad.

It had happened: the love of my life was pregnant. It was completely unexpected, unplanned and accidental. Although I had always harboured the desire for a child, I didn't think it would really seriously happen. I was as shocked as Chloe. How the hell had it happened? I knew how it happened physically, but we had always been careful. Chloe was horrified and I felt guilty for a crime I hadn't committed. I'd had my chances in the past and they were taken away. My new life, which was devoted to my wife, was totally built on the understanding that children weren't part of the plan. I understood and accepted it. Mostly because she didn't think she was the maternal type but also because she had never really wanted children. I knew the thought scared her. She knew she was different; she had been brought up to think they weren't important.

Selfishly, I guess part of me had hoped that once married, settled and happy she might change her mind, and this to some extent had happened as she had made some positive noises, saying that in the right circumstances she might actually consider children. Every positive murmur caused a little hope in my heart, although I was happy as we were.

But unfortunately we weren't settled: we were living in rented accommodation whilst trying to find a home. We both had properties that were being rented, although my wife had been unfortunate with her tenant and had to go to court to get her house back. This delay put paid to

35

us finding a home of our own when we most needed it.

We were also deep in the recession and job prospects weren't great. Holding on to our jobs was proving tough in itself, let alone seeking new challenges.

I found my Grandad in a side room with my mum and dad sitting silently by his bedside. They both looked utterly knackered; he had only just fallen asleep. He was my last remaining grandparent and was in the same hospital I never saw my Nan leave. My Grandad, and my hero.

Two years after my Nan had died and having learnt to be self-sufficient again, something in his brain had given way and he'd suffered some sort of blood clot. Being made of strong stuff and although suffering stroke-like symptoms, he was still busy trying to rip out his drip and catheter as soon as he woke up. He didn't care that he couldn't speak or swallow, he just didn't want to be in bed any more. It was the worst day of my life having to help restrain him in hospital; I just wanted to take him home. I didn't have a chance to tell him my news.

My buttons were being pushed.

Grandad normally would have wanted to know all about my work. I could have told him about Chloe and the baby and all about my troubles, no matter how trivial. Even if he couldn't do much about them, he always seemed to know how to make them go away.

I tried to tell him. In my head on the train back to London I told him over and over again. In between thoughts of him struggling to get out of bed and his utter confusion and Chloe's look of pure terror as she said 'I'm pregnant', the countryside gave way to London town.

17 – POLO'S AND DONUTS

I'D DECIDED STUD EARRINGS looked rubbish on lads. If I got myself a hoop I could save myself the hassle and just sort it out myself. Apparently high street jewellers insisted on you wearing a stud first before you were able to be promoted to the hoop-wearing brigade. I was sure that this was simply a con.

Getting the earring was the easy part of my plan; getting it through my ear lobe was going to be the tricky part.

First off, I put ice in the freezer. I was going to utilise the tried and tested technique that all old ladies like my Nan said their mums had used before the war. It shouldn't be too hard, I thought: a bit of ice on the lobe, pin at the ready. I had already watched the pin glow as I heated it on the gas hob; I knew this was the best way to sterilise it but hadn't anticipated the burnt fingers. I put the ice cube on my ear and looked at myself in the mirror. *Here we go.* I took the ice cube away from my ear; water was dripping from my wrist. I thought my ear would feel number than it did. *Okay, here we go,* I thought...

Fuck that feels weird! A sort of stinging and crunching sensation as the pin gradually pierced the flesh. I could feel the tip of the pin on my thumb and knew I just needed to push it through the last little bit. The pin was completely through. When I pulled it out I got the hoop ready. I decided I'd put it straight through and the job was done, easy, or so I thought. As I pulled the pin out of my already bright red, burning ear, I grabbed the hoop and tried to put it through the hole... no good. It started stinging like hell and bleeding. *Great, I proper fucked that up.*

I thought I'd best have a re-think sharpish.

I decided the best thing to do was increase the size of the pin to a needle and this time properly freeze my ear. My plan this time was to freeze some wet tissue paper. That way I could hold more freezing

37

material on my ear for longer. Sweet, it was working fine: my ear had stopped bleeding and my lobe was feeling absolutely numb and I was ready again with the needle. I was sure I could definitely have found something not quite as drastic size wise between the pin and the needle, but in the end opted for Henry the VIII's old lance. The needle went in fairly painlessly, but again I felt odd as I heard the stretching and cracking ear tissue and flesh being slowly torn, but the needle was through nevertheless. I kept pulling until the needle was literally at the halfway point. The sharp point touched my neck and the eye end stuck out nicely like an antenna.

I thought I looked the nuts, so I left it for a while as I admired my handiwork in several mirrors from every conceivable angle, in every room in our house. I was trying to determine just how good it really looked... more punk than casual, I decided, although I still felt it was highly unlikely that the hoop would look much better.

But when I finally went to remove the needle I realised my ear was no longer frozen and the internal fibres and blood had congealed and bonded to the metal needle. It had well and truly set. As I tugged on the needle my ear started bleeding again, then throbbing and then I felt quite sick as the pain kicked in. When the needle was completely free I could see I had created a perfect hole and put the hoop through very tentatively but successfully.

My problem now was hiding the earring from my family. I reckoned my sisters would be impressed, but knew my parents would think I looked like an idiot and school would also not approve. I felt this was best overcome with a disguise. I decided to wear a cap and brush my hair over my ears. Problem solved: no one need ever know I had an earring.

18 – IS IT WRONG?

I WAS SITTING WITH GRANDAD in the hospital. The lights were on but no one was in. I held his hand and stroked his head, looking into his eyes for a glimmer of recognition.

'I want to take you home, Grandad, have a nice cup of tea.'

I could almost hear him reply in my head. He didn't move, he just nattered away to himself, more incomprehensible nonsense.

'It's hot in here, isn't it, Grandad? Why's it so flippin' hot? Your cucumbers would grow in here alright, wouldn't they, mate? It's like your greenhouse!' I tried to say the sort of thing that would have made him laugh. He always laughed at my jokes.

It was so hot I couldn't breathe. Why was there no air? Should I open a window? Would he get cold? I didn't know what to do or say any more. I knew what I wanted to ask. Was it wrong to expect your other half to be there for you when you felt like you were falling apart? Was it something you were supposed to understand and look for before you got married? Potential weaknesses and all that... should you already know that if you're emotional or struggling then the reassuring hands and shoulders to cry on might not be those of the person you're relying on? Was this how affairs started? Was it fair to say that no one knows anything and you're lucky to find someone who's always there? A better person than you who somehow telepathically understands what you're feeling?

I felt like I was there for everyone. A natural empathy, like a noose around my neck, always burdened with others' problems. I always offered my services; my two penn'th worth came free. Was that the deal breaker? Was I chosen as the husband for that reason? Because I'd be there when needed and easily ignored when the tables were turned? Was I wrong to think this? Was I being selfish now?

My Grandad was hurting, confused and alone in hospital. I wasn't sure what he could feel any more. It hurt me to see him like that. I'd comfort him, like I'd want someone to comfort me. Should I feel bad for wanting him to either live or die at the same moment? Would she understand me thinking this? Did she know I was thinking this? Why didn't she have the answers?

What am I supposed to do, Grandad? Will she terminate our baby? My job's shit, Grandad. I can't give her what she wants. Talk to me, Grandad. Give me the answers, please. What should I do?

19 – FIESTA SIESTA

'THE REAL THING' WAS BLARING OUT of the stereo. Sarah and Neil and I all sang along as loudly as we could. We had just entered the roundabout at Blackmore. I was driving the love wagon. Just another teenage turbo GT Nutter bastard. The motor did zero to sixty in about fourteen seconds. On paper it was just another blue Fiesta. Distinguishing features: it had one black door and a stereo with serious treble action. When I had Josh Wink's 'Higher state of consciousness' playing, humming birds in Madagascar thought a forest fire was approaching from the north. On the official documents it boasted a 950cc engine, but when I hit a tonne the speedo bounced. I was convinced it was at least a 1300cc; either that or the old fella I'd bought it off had been an old racing driver and had tuned the beast up. When I put the pedal to the metal daisies on the side of the road took a mild buffering.

As I exited the roundabout, heading for Sarah's house, Neil said, 'I think I just saw a cop car.'

Shit, I thought, *best step on the gas and lose them.*

It was one long, straight road, they had a car capable of zero to sixty in less than seven seconds, I had a couple of hundred metres head start and, with a good wind and a freak lightning strike, a fair to no chance at all of outrunning them. Undeterred, I engaged warp factor nothing and watched the speedo creep surreptitiously towards forty-five miles per hour. I was fairly certain the back roads around that area had sixty-miles-per-hour speed limits; if we had caught the fuzz's attention it was most likely due to us singing loudly rather than my erratic or erotic driving. There was no doubt the pigs were on my tail; I was nearly up to fifty-five miles per hour and running out of road. They probably hadn't anticipated my knowledge of the local roads; shit, they could have mistaken me for an old lady up until that point.

The road ended at a T-junction. It was a forty-five-degree right-hand turn and then straight away a left-hand turn, bearing into Sarah's road, another country lane, and a hundred or so metres further along was my fail safe, get-out-of-jail-free card... my *pièce de résistance* would come into play: the conifer-lined driveway to her house. If judged correctly I could turn off my lights and pull into the driveway, leaving the Ice Poles completely flummoxed and in the dark as to where I had disappeared to.

That was the plan. I didn't really have time to run it past Sarah and Neil; they would just have to be accessories. I hadn't really given it much thought myself. I just went for it.

The first right went okay. It was dark and I could see that no headlights were coming in either direction. It would have been deemed bad driving to everyone but any seventeen-year-old anywhere in the world or a trainee getaway driver. They at least would have admired the cornering capabilities of yours truly in my Fiesta 1.3 meat injection.

Unfortunately the plod weren't impressed or easily shaken. I took the right and left turnings, barely touching the brake and using the full amount of road. Neil nearly spilt his Tango. I motored up to the conifers that led to Sarah's house and hit the lights just as I'd planned in my head only seconds earlier. Just as my lights went out the blue flashing lights came on. Busted. Game over.

Neil and Sarah went silent in the car; they expected me to do bird on their account. I wasn't going down like that, though; they weren't going to lock me up and throw away the key. I stopped the car and waited for the five o's to get out. I thought about flooring it again like they do in the movies just as the rozzers get out. I decided I'd been caught and would take my punishment like a man.

'Fuck me, he's huge.'

The tallest policeman I'd ever seen walked up to the car. He nearly had to kneel down to look through the window. When he did he looked straight at Sarah, fleetingly; a look of recognition. He tapped the window and asked me to step out of the vehicle.

'Why were you in such a rush, eh?' he said.

'I wanted to get her home,' I said, looking at Sarah in the car.

'You should be more careful with a lovely young lady like that in your car,' he said. *Oh no, he fancies Sarah*, I thought.

'I thought you might be the bummers,' I said.

'Excuse me?' he said.

'You know, those dodgy blokes dressed up like police who've been carrying out those heinous crimes against innocent members of the community, Officer. You can't trust anyone, and Neil in the car is always having strange blokes look at him in a suggestive manner, Officer.'

Neil just sat and stared aimlessly out the window.

'I see,' the policeman said, looking at Neil, almost momentarily sensing his vulnerability.

'How's the car going?' he asked, throwing me off track suddenly.

'Okay,' I said, thinking, *It corners like it's on rails actually, mate, you were lucky you could keep up with me. If I didn't have these two weighing me down I'd be out of here.*

'Only I helped do it up!'

'You what'?

'You purchased it from Old Mick who lives opposite me. I helped tune it up and get it on the road, and you got a good motor there.'

'Blimey,' I said, thinking, *Should I ask what size engine it really had?* 'You must be Big Ron's dad. I know your son: he's a friend of mine, and we go to college together.'

He said, 'I know Sarah's family as well, and you should take more care driving young ladies around.' He didn't seem to care too much about Neil any more. 'Let this be a warning to you. Have a good night, and be more careful in future, young man,' he said, getting back in the cop car.

You be careful, I thought, *there are dangerous bummers out there.*

20 – DIMINISHING

I WAS SITTING ON MY OWN in the pub at Marylebone station, just staring at my half-full pint of Guinness. Two packets of peanuts, one dry roasted, the other salty, were going to be my dinner for tonight. A red-haired couple sat canoodling in the corner, both sporting similar pierced faces and big woolly cardigans; all wrapped up warm in thick scarves and heavy boots, all snugly and loved up. I felt jealous of their tenderness and affection.

Were diminishing responsibilities enough reason to commit crime? Did life's negative experiences warrant sudden bad behaviour? Was it greed or anger or hurt that suddenly made you a bad person? When did a good person become bad? Could taking drugs at some point in your life lead to you to become someone who committed a premeditated action? Would that be an excuse? Could doing drugs once or twice damage your brain to the extent that you became a bad person? Would losing loved ones or job pressures or moving house create enough stress that a certain person might react by doing certain drastic actions? What would be the point of stealing or causing pain? What would the benefit be to me? Would my life be better? Would the fear or reality of losing everything be enough of an incentive to go out and cause mayhem? How far would most people go? Would spreading myself too thin and losing my job and perhaps everything else I hold dear to me be enough of a reason to take action? Would that be the catalyst: a new house, a lovely wife, a family? All gone, how should I cope? I coped before; I could cope again couldn't I? It was different now; I didn't want to cope any more.

Could it just be in my nature? As an innocent kid I'd got up to mischief; perhaps now as an adult my horizons had broadened and so had my levels of mayhem. Perhaps some people never grew up; I was quite sure as an adult I'd been told I needed to. I remembered my Mum used to say, 'Only the innocent get caught.' Perhaps I'd got away with too much or perhaps I just did what I did because I could and wanted to.

Did this make me a bad person, or was I simply one of life's opportunists?

21 – THE CROSS AND BLACKWALL

WE'D ORGANISED A PARTY BUS to take our group of mates from Essex to The Cross in King's Cross and back home again in the morning. Martin and I had taken charge of the party prescriptions. Unbeknownst to us, it was the same day as Gay Pride.

I'd recently split up with Sarah but neither of us had any intention of missing the night out. We all had on our best dancing clobber and were ready and waiting for a proper shindig. The coach journey on the way up to London was collectively exciting, almost hopeful. I found myself seeking out Sarah's eye, hoping to make contact. Despite the butterflies in my stomach part of me hoped the night might end with us making up; stranger things had happened and I missed her for sure.

When we left the coach and made our way to the queue, Martin and I became nervous over the security on the door and the full-on shoe-removal-style body searches being carried out on the clubbers in front of us. We noticed the eagle-eyed doorman noticing us noticing his security measures at the same moment. We'd never make it through, so we switched to Plan C. We left the rapidly shortening line and went for a wander around the block.

'Shit, that was close. What are we going to do, man?' Martin looked at me, hoping I had a plan.

'We should have sold it earlier,' I said, not helping matters. 'How about we stick the stuff down our pants?' I suggested, knowing I had dodgy boxers on and thinking that would mean Martin would have to take the stuff.

No good, he was going commando.

'Shit.'

We had no idea how to hide the pink champagne, and neither of us could see a secure enough place to try stashing it either.

'Fuck it, let's just do it all,' I said.

'All of it? Won't we overdose, dude?' Martin replied.

'Can you overdose on speed?'

'I don't know.'

'What's the most anyone's ever done in one go?'

'I don't know.'

'Fuck it, let's do it.'

The two of us went for it, tearing open the little paper wraps, joining one per cent of the world's population, living and dead – hard-core caners, rockers and ravers and speed queens. Certainly not many had lived to tell the tale, not that we knew of anyway. Three and a half grams each gone in a matter of seconds. Fingers rapidly rubbing powder into our gums.

Never before had I wanted a drink so badly. Semi-gagging, convulsing, smoking! Doing absolutely anything at all to take away the foul taste. All I wanted was an orange squash or a scouring brush for my tongue. Battery acid would have tasted great right then. I wanted so badly to stop swallowing.

'How're you feeling, Martin?'

'Fine. You?' he said, lying.

'Yeah, great thanks,' I replied.

'Another ciggy?' Martin asked.

'Yeah, why the hell not?' I said, bravado overflowing.

Now, I should have told the truth, but that was hardly going to help the situation – admitting anything was bad could cause a spiralling negative effect and right now we needed to be positive. So we were both lying to each other. P.M.A. Positive Mental Attitude. Negative could come later; we needed to get into the club first. We weren't ready for the comedown yet; hells bells, we weren't even ready for the take-off. Jesus wept, Christ on a bike, we weren't even at the launch pad yet either. We had to get a wriggle on.

We got back to the club in no time at all; we were almost panting, having jogged most the way. The overly observant security bloke called us over to be searched.

'You alright?' he asked semi-suspiciously.

'Yeah, you?' I replied, staring him hard in the eyes, concentrating on controlling my gag reflex, desperate to not start gulping or looking nervous or saying anything stupid.

'Where'd you run off to?' he asked.

'I needed some cash, mate,' I said, patting my wallet as if to emphasise my point, illustrating that it was now bulging with crisp new notes still warm and straight from the machine.

'Let's see,' he said, beckoning for my wallet. 'Also take off your shoes and lift your arms, please, mate.' He checked my wallet; it contained my last twenty pounds in cash in the world, four virgin five pound notes, and no drugs. He checked my fags, chewing gum packet, shoes and socks, and thoroughly patted me down as well.

'Bend down, please, mate.'

'Are you serious?'

'Nahhhh, only joking with ya, mate.'

Had his reply taken one second longer I'd have been well on my way to exposing my rusty sheriff's badge without a moment's thought.

'Are you with those girls that were in the queue earlier in front of you like, you know, the pretty little blonde ones with the lovely jugs, little sort, blonde hair, right?' the bald-headed, spade-handed, gold-tooth-sporting, double-hard, funny-man, eagle-eyed, chatter-box new-best-mate with a serious steroid problem asked with a wiggle of the eyebrows and a filthy look of mischievousness that suggested nothing but menace.

'Erm yeah, why?'

'Oh, no reason, have fun.'

What the fuck does that mean? I thought.

Martin got through the intense grilling as well and we made our way into the club. I drank a beer then some water like a seriously thirsty camel. Like a camel that was so thirsty from eating nothing but sand and crackers for months on end that all its humps and shit had withered to sacks of skin like old sacks used at school for sack races.

I didn't feel like talking, I felt like dancing. I was jittering like a baby gazelle on a roasting tray covered in rosemary and baked in the oven at two hundred degrees and served with meaty, hot, red wine gravy; just how Mrs Lion and all her family like it. Mmmm.

Once the thirst was partially quenched, the music, which incidentally was the most banging house music I'd ever heard and could only be resisted by the completely deaf and dumb or people absolutely devoid of any musical appreciation... *Oh my God, I just have to dance!* With a bottle of water in my hand, the stage beckoned. I was sucked towards the centre; everywhere it seemed people were dancing in slow motion. I had time to move to each and every individual beat. Every change in melody and rhythm I could reflect with a flick of the wrist or waggle of the finger. I was the lord of dance. I was the greatest dancer. I had hours and lifetimes between beats, every bassy burping sound setting me off on more manic fluid movements. That's when it passed me: the seven foot condom, enjoying Gay Pride no doubt. Still, no time to jibber jabber, especially not with a huge prophylactic. *I just got to dance.* I would have tiggled his ribs but didn't fancy getting mud under my nails. I powered on, oblivious to anyone or anything. I wasn't moving from my stage and everyone in the club knew that was my space now. I was conducting the orchestra; I had a bottle of water. I had no need for anything else in the world apart from a continuous stream of cigarettes. The music was so perfect. 'Let's have it!' I screamed whilst whooping like a Red Indian, focusing on nothing but the dancing and the tunes.

Then it was over. 'What do you mean we're leaving? We've only just got here.'

I couldn't believe I'd been dancing nonstop for seven hours and the bus had returned to take us home: next stop Essex, but not before stopping by Comedown city en route.

We clambered aboard the mentalist bus; I was a certified window licker for sure. I could hear Sarah chatting and laughing at the rear of the bus. I had hardly seen her all night; I guessed she had been avoiding me – perhaps she had been with the bouncer who'd seemed so interested. They would have made a lovely couple and have had lots of amazing sex.

I put my head against the damp, cold glass window and the condensation gathered on my squalid skin. The engine and road vibrations massaged my throbbing brain, my clothes were wet through with sweat and I was cold now, wide awake yet utterly shattered. All I could hear was Sarah laughing and having fun with her girlfriends. It was dawn and my heart was beating like a metronome attached to an amp. What had happened to the night? Who had sped up the clocks and stolen my time? I felt like I'd only been in the club for half an hour, and why the hell was Sarah having so much fun? I'd definitely been cheated. I looked around the bus for Martin, sticking my head up out of my trench like a meercat momentarily. He too looked like he had been dealt a rough hand in a deal with the devil, like a solider battle-scarred and under siege, like some beaten, screwed-up rouge trader, like a beaten chess player, like a fucked-up, disco-dancing druggy!

22 – GATE CRASHER

JAMES AND I WERE MAKING the most of having a night off from the wives. James' sister was in the music business; she was married to a manager also in the business. James' brother Neil was also in a band. I had been in it for a while as well, at least many years ago, when he was first starting out. I was the bongo player and driver and occasional backing singer. We sang songs by groups like Boys to Men and Extreme; not really my thing at all. We recorded a few tracks we'd written but they were fairly crap, apart from the bongo section at least.

We had gone to see James' brother's band play and now we were at an after-show party hosted by his sister's record company. It was a family affair. It turned out to be a right old mish mash of who's who in the celebrity world and a blend of the current cool crowd. Apparently Kate Moss, Russell Brand and Kate Perry, Paulo Nutini and Noel Gallagher from Oasis were there, but I didn't see any of them. I did see the orange face of Dale Winton, though. Perhaps I missed the 'A-listers' because I was too busy staggering from the free bar to the dance floor and the toilet and back.

We were in a dark wooden bar with flashes of blue neon. Scantily clad women and younger girls trying to look older and acting miserable to seem sophisticated were two a penny. I got the impression there was a heavy security presence although the door was your usual bouncer affair. Strange suited blokes wearing shades and discreet earpieces stood in dark corners, not dealing just looking. James pointed out some sultan of somewhere or other; word had it that his hired entourage of ladies were adorned in rented, priceless jewels, usually saved for red carpet dos, but here in the club tonight they were just reflecting his money and the blue neon and bling. I guessed the security was his, or the jewels'. He looked like he'd need protecting more than the girls with the jewels. I wouldn't have fancied taking on one of the mini-skirted golems in an attempt to part her from her precious diamond ring.

James said the sultan was known to let his hair down at these parties but no photos of his drinking could ever find their way into the public arena. Super injunctions were taken out with all the press just in case, and it was probably a racist's argument fuelled by a tabloid article waiting to happen along the lines of 'it's all right for them to come over here and do it', but there he was, as pissed as a fart. I bumped into him on the way out of the toilet. I didn't much care for his attitude; nor he much for mine. He looked at me with distaste; I looked at him with pity. One of his bouncers pushed me away and I called him a prick. I didn't think any more of it until James found me and said I'd been asked to leave. The sultan's men must have said something to James' sister's employers because she seemed to have the right hump with me as well. I told them I hadn't done anything but that didn't seem to matter.

I got my coat from the cloakroom and slumped out of the club. The cab home cost eighty-five quid and Chloe got in a strop with me for waking her up and then the cat went mental and refused to sleep all night, jumping on and off the bed, and when I shut it out of the room it sat outside meowing and scratching the carpet and door.

23 – HELP

I SAT NEXT TO LOUISE on the bed. We'd become good friends since our first day at college. She reminded me of a lovely little mouse: she was very English, charming and strangely London countrified. I think her mum must have been some sort of hippy. She didn't want to get involved in the ouija board stuff either.

We were on a week-long college trip to Paris, by day taking in the usual touristy sights like the Eiffel Tower, the Louvre, the Pompadom Centre and the Sucre Coeur, and by night getting drunk and stoned while the lecturers tried their luck with the vulnerable.

A group of students invaded my room, a damp, spacious number with high ceilings, dim lights, dirty linen and a view over a Parisian crossroads on a slight hill with other French looking B&Bs, all squalid and cold, and of course spitting distance from the red light area. The air was thick with cheap dope smuggled into France in socks, duty-free fags chain smoked and JD fumes of young, over-confident measures.

We had spent all day in the cold, drizzly, grey November conditions trying to find Jim Morrison's grave. I wouldn't have minded so much but I didn't even like The Doors that much. When we made our way back to the hotel we soon learnt which bar the rest of the students had taken over. It was always the same one I had sorted out on the first night and the barman welcomed me in like an old friend, giving me drinks on the house. I guess having one hundred students turning up throughout the day and night for a week was a most unexpected boost for the French bar steward's coffers. By allowing us free use of the jukebox we also created an atmosphere that for most of the year was presumably missing. I had hoped that my decision to use his bar somehow meant the place had transformed and become a 'spot' in Paris. Certainly Parisians joined us for an impromptu rave up after we arrived. I figured I would be quite good at that business.

We all got drunk and after a while noisily went back to our hotel. Louise and I sat on the bed watching the group conspire like demented witches around a cauldron. Possibly due to the smoke and booze the room already had an atmosphere before Carol, the self-appointed master of ceremonies, began the usual ritual.

'Is there anybody there?'

The group gathered around the green, felt-topped table on an assortment of chairs, leaning forward with fingers all placed on top of the glass surrounded by letters and numbers and 'YES' and 'NO' spelt out on pieces of paper.

A couple of times they had tried to make contact: six people crowded around a little table with fingers poised, others leant over shoulders checking for skulduggery, whilst a few skulked in the background getting stoned.

'I don't like this,' I said to Louise.

'Me neither,' she meekly replied.

The glass wobbled a fraction and the room came alive with evil electricity as a buzz enveloped the room. I picked up a discarded plastic fork someone had used for woofing down some French fries covered in tomato ketchup, and started nervously, semi-consciously, fiddling to distract my sweating hands and nervous mind.

'Did it move?' I asked Louise.

'I think it did,' she said, even more mouse-like than ever before almost squeaking. I stared at the group's faces; a nervous nasty grin was etched on Steve's, concentration on others. Apprehension filled the air. I could feel Louise fidgeting beside me; her anxiety was catching and I continued absentmindedly playing with the plastic fork.

The glass shuddered towards 'YES'. Somebody was there or here or wherever ghosts hung out. The smoke in the room began to move more like waves in the room, as if ghostly apparitions were joining us in our little dingy, dimly lit French hovel. The dim sidelight cast a faint, warm glow.

'Who are you?' the chief instigator asked.

The glass slowly spelt out the name 'Nicole'.

'How old are you, Nicole?'

Nicole was twelve; Nicole was a little Parisian girl.

'How did you die?'

'Daddy' was the answer.

'Did your Daddy kill you, Nicole?'

'Yes.'

My fingers went into overdrive, furiously fiddling with the plastic fork. I wasn't enjoying this. Nicole was murdered by her father, and further questions revealed her mummy was in danger. The glass spelt out a succession of letters that meant little to anyone in the room, and when the ring leader said he didn't understand the spelling became quicker and faster, over and over again.

A I D E A I D E A I D E A I D E A I D E

The glass moved across the table like an invisible hand was guiding it. The group spelt out the letters in unison, almost chanting monk-like until Louise screamed.

'It means "help" in French. She's asking for your help!'

All the hands broke off the glass simultaneously, and everyone in the room sat transfixed momentarily by the table, except Louise. She shuffled forward off the bed, briefly touching my hand; she couldn't stand any more and said she was going to bed. I walked out into the corridor with her to check she was okay.

'I'm sorry, I really don't like that sort of thing,' she said.

'Err, don't worry, Lou, it scares the shit out of me as well,' I replied.

'What's that in your hand?' she asked, looking down at the fork I'd been fidgeting with. It no longer looked like a fork; it had been perfectly ripped to shreds and woven to create the form of a crucifix.

'Blimey, I don't know, I guess I made it whilst all that was going on. I didn't realise I was making it. I certainly didn't mean to. Do you want it?' I asked, thinking my amazing transformation might be good luck or protection or something.

Louise smiled, touched my arm again and said. 'Tell you the truth, they freak me out as well. Night then, I'll be alright.'

Then she was gone, like a little mouse back into her hole. I sort of wished I could go with her and curl up like a little mouse too; she seemed so clean, pure and innocent. Instead I had to go back to my room, the den of inequity where evil lurked in every corner and filth oozed from every crevice. Still, I had my crucifix for protection.

I went back into the room, where Mel had taken my place on the bed. Bloody hell, beautiful Mel! Things might be alright after all. She shuffled up so I could squeeze in next to her and passed me a half-smoked joint, still wet from her lips. Mel was gorgeous, a beautiful blonde in the Kate Moss or Vanessa Paradise mould, like an angel but sexy in an unassuming way. It was a damn shame her best mate at college had claimed me; it kind of threw a spanner in the works totally.

I sat there, joint in hand, wisps from my smoke joining the ghostly clouds moving like apparitions entering the fray. Carol, my witch of a girlfriend, started up again.

'Is there anyone there?'

We all sat around waiting for the next spectacle. The whole table shook, like someone had walked up and kicked the table. I shook, the whole room shook, evil, evil was amongst us. All the witches backed away from the table bar Steve. Steve, the crazy, angry alcoholic schitzo hippy, calmly turned over the glass they had been using as the tool on the ouija board, filled it with JD and drank down the spirit; his soul was eternally cursed and damaged anyway. I got up and put my plastic crucifix in his empty glass and dropped both in the straw bin in the corner of the room.

24 – RYAN

A GOOD FRIEND RYAN worked for an art insurance firm dealing in fine art. I worked for a printer printing any and every printed item imaginable. Sometimes our worlds collided. I happened to notice a document we'd produced on behalf of Ryan's company; the document mentioned a high profile client that I had also recently had the pleasure of briefly meeting.

That's the thing about printing: sometimes you notice things or are in the position to read strictly private and confidential documents.

It became apparent that Mr Sultan of wherever, who lived not far from Little Venice, off Regent's Canal, had recently purchased a priceless painting and due to insufficient security was being refused insurance. It seemed the company advisors felt sticking a priceless Picasso amongst countless other masterpieces on the lounge wall, not far from the kitchen, overlooking the garden, wasn't the most secure of plans, and thus felt it wouldn't be an installation they could back or insure. Also listed were the names of several other insurance companies that would also share a similar view.

That man surely did have more money than sense. The fact that a member of staff was usually in the house all the time and he had a burglar alarm did little to sway the insurance companies. They expected twenty-four-hour CCTV and bullet-proof glass and proper security measures.

It didn't really matter to me, although a seed had been sown.

I was being threatened with redundancy as the company figures were so bad, although mine personally were okay-ish, at least not far off my projected targets; it was the big hitters, the top salesman, who were really letting the company down. Unfortunately being younger than my colleagues, the statutory payments necessary to lay me off were far less than some of my more senior and inept colleagues. I'd already had to accept a fifteen per cent pay cut; annoying as I hadn't been given a pay rise for years and years, and if I was to give Chloe all the things she wanted, pay cuts weren't the right way to be heading for sure.

I couldn't bring myself to tell her. Bastards everywhere were dragging me down and fucking me up. Chloe felt I should have demanded a rise, and mentioned more than once perhaps it was worth looking for a new job. I wasn't a quitter, though. If I'd been a professional footballer I'd have been a one club type. I wanted to earn my respect where I worked rather than moving to seek the respect elsewhere. Perhaps she thought they saw me as a mug and I was blind to it.

I just wanted to get on with our lives like every other couple seemed to do. Go to work, build a nest, have a family? Settle down, get old and die happily. I was struggling with every hurdle; I was stuck in a chimney, in a maze, down a one-way road.

25 – SAVE ME

IT WAS THE DAY BEFORE NEW YEAR'S EVE and we were heading home after a forty-eight-hour party session in Madchester. Pills had been popped like they were going out of fashion. James had DJ'd at a party and we had faithfully accompanied him as chief support dancers and gurners. I wondered whether I had chosen this role for my life or had it thrust upon me. There was little doubt I was great at it; it certainly took someone special. Often I'd assist his set by becoming a bongo bashing pilled-up madman; like many other nights my fingers would end the session wrapped in plasters as I'd play until they bled.

For the drive back south we had packed Nick's car with the records and decks and piled in. Me, James and his girlfriend Emma in the back; Nick and his mate Tom in the front. We barely made it five metres before my mind drifted into a comedown-induced lull. It had been barely a half an hour earlier that I'd been found sitting upright under a bundle of people's clothes, trying to get warm and comfortable. Half an hour before that I'd been wandering the streets of Manchester as high as a kite and completely lost, having climbed out of the window several hours earlier.

I took on the role as chief window licker; not for the first time my face was chilled by the condensation on the glass. My eyes were distracted by the orange glow from street lights and the warm orbs and beams chucked out from passing cars. The drizzle from the damp, wet northern night aided my muzzy-headed state. As the tunes on the stereo progressed they locked into my brain's internal workings and realigned my chilled-out state. Occasional uplifting beats wrestled with my fatigued being and semiconscious mind, nudging it from its slumbering, resigned state. The motorways lines drummed out a monotonous pattern in my head. Everyone in the car was alone with their thoughts, running on empty, barely alive. Emma broke that calm by screaming:

'Nick! Look out!'

Our designated driver for the return journey had drifted off; we were accelerating out of the middle lane and gaining quickly on the car in the outside fast lane. As Emma yelped we were collectively torn from our slumber just in time to see Nick react. His natural instinct was possibly the same as anyone's when confronted with the rear of a car not going as fast as yours: it was to steer back towards the middle lane, away from trouble. Unfortunately his reaction was too wild and didn't take into consideration the cold, wet, icy evening, or the eighty-miles-per-hour velocity we must have been exceeding. As soon as his left-hand-down manoeuvre had corrected itself we entered into a spin. James and I put our arms across the middle of the partition in the rear of the car to act as some sort of safety net for Emma should she be launched from her seat and out of the window. We'd seen the TV adverts and subconsciously hoped our arms might stop her flying through the air. I'm sure they would have shattered anyway, but it was a good thought and James and I had thought it at the same moment.

As we span like a waltzer at the fairground, at least three times we went round, the car clipped the inner lane's reservation and we then seemed to straighten out. We knew straight away something was still wrong. Headlights were shining in our direction and we were still hurtling along.

We were going backwards, still at an incredible rate of knots. Nick's first reaction was to turn the steering wheel and again we launched into another set of break-neck spins. We all screamed in unison. It was an euphoric, almost slow motion sensation of relaxed inevitability. We could do nothing about the situation but enjoy the ride, pirouetting around and around. Lights flashing, petrified grimaces on faces almost strobing in the reflections.

We clipped the outer reservation and came to a sliding halt. The car was facing the wrong way up the motorway. The hazard lights of drivers approaching us changed our immediate view with the orange lights joining the full beams to warn other road users of our and their immediate peril. The middle lane traffic came to a halt first, giving my spinning head something to focus on as a non-moving entity. I breathed again as cars in the fast lane skidded to a pedestrian pace.

We sat in silence, just staring, the windscreen wipers monotonously burping out disgruntled murmurs of damp condemnation: squelch burp, squelch burp, squelch burp, squelch burp. I noticed the little drops of rain fighting the battle with the wipers then heard the music still coming from the stereo. It seemed to vanish from my ears and then come back just so I'd notice its tune. Faithless, 'Save Me'; that struck me as a little ironic.

'Are you, err, you alright?' I asked Emma.

'Yeah, you?' she said, looking at James, not an ounce of emotion on anyone's face.

James carried it on. 'You alright, Nick?'

Nick carried it on, looking at Tom.

Everyone was fine. Through the collective sighs I figured the lottery of life had deemed our numbers were good; either that or divine intervention had kept the wheels on the ground. Truth be told, I never thought I'd die, although as we clambered out of the car unscathed it was clear the car was a total right-off. James was a relieved man to see his records and decks had somehow survived as well. The front and back of the car were totally smashed up and one wheel was hanging off.

As we gingerly climbed out of the car and into the freezing, wet drizzle and scurried up the side of a hill that ran alongside the motorway, James pointed and said, 'Shit, look at that.' As we looked we could see other crashes on the other side of the motorway; on the other carriage rubber-neckers were getting totalled in the carnage we'd caused. Still, we had New Year's Eve to look forward to.

26 – I COULD LEAVE

I ALWAYS SEEMED TO BE JUST SITTING at my desk, minute by minute, never-ending daydreams, staring at my silhouette in my computer screen. My brain was working overtime, over-stretched and no longer thinking day to day but minute by minute, searching for excuses, plans and possibilities. I must find an escape.

I began ignoring my friends' emails, texts and messages. I didn't want anyone's help or support or suggestions on how I should live my life. At least at work I could bury my head in the sand. Although I didn't live to work, when life outside work became a grind, it was a lot easier working to live.

I found myself thinking I could leave my bike at Marylebone station; it was safe there, inconspicuous amongst thousands of others. I'd left it there before, on platform three, and it had been there the next day even though I'd left it unlocked at the time, in too much of a rush to make the train, when I was busy rushing to see Grandad or Chloe in hospital. There weren't many places in London that was possible. It was secure and I could get to it any time the trains were running and the station was open. All I needed was my Oyster card, and I could then get anywhere else in London. I could use the trains from there in an emergency to get almost anywhere in the country or even the world.

I could ride from Marylebone to King's Cross in rush hour in about ten minutes. I could get to the city itself in half an hour and the West End in twenty minutes and West London in quarter of an hour. East London would take a while longer.

I'd rented space at places before like Big Yellow and other companies that offer you a protected lock-up. All services could be pre-paid and there at my disposal.

I didn't like the idea of getting buses anywhere; they were too bright and too slow and in your face. Everyone has seen the scary man on the bus before.

27 – LIE CHESTER SQUARE

PATRICK AND I HAD BEEN DRINKING in a few bars and clubs around Leicester Square. We had been involved in a minor altercation earlier in the evening with some pissed-up northerners which resulted in them bottling it. Although there were five of them and only two of us, it was Patrick's effect not mine; he could have dealt with all five of them with little bother. I was nothing more than a lad who'd recently left art college and Pat was a self-confessed armed robber, coke and pill dealer and double-hard bastard. He had an Irish mum and West Indian dad and his missus was beautiful and he had a lovely baby daughter and some strange connection to the band Erasure that I never really understood; either way, he was my mate. I liked the way he liked everyone to a certain point and even if someone was as camp as Christmas he'd like them as long as 'they didn't try to bum me'.

This would explain the reason we walked half the way through Soho as bold as brass chatting with a load of fully dressed up transvestites. Usually I'd be like everyone else, pointing and giggling and not saying boo to a goose or duck, but with Pat it was different. We laughed and chatted with everyone, even the trannies, like old friends.

We went into a bustling pub on the edge of Covent Garden. The smell of piss filled your lungs as soon as you entered the building. The place was hundreds of years old. Bare fist fighting used to happen there, and we were enjoying the reminiscing when someone passing through asked if we'd like to buy some weed. I gave Pat some money and we left the pub. I was in a bit of a daze and not sure if we were following anyone in the busy late evening commuter chaos.

We entered a club by going down some stairs, and we were now in deepest, darkest seedy Soho, back when you smoked in pubs. There were Irish fellas singing IRA songs and playing Rastas at pool. One Rasta made a cut throat sign at me. I checked behind me, hoping someone would be there. Fuck, I was just another art bum college boy wearing a black sheepskin coat with brown fur lining with blue jeans and white trainers on. What the fuck had I done to upset him? Was it my Liam Gallagher style mop, still refusing to believe or submit to the inherited inevitable receding hairline? My pasty white face? What the fuck had I done? I wasn't offensive to look at and I wasn't racist: I didn't dislike Rastas; I had a Bob Marley album and everything.

The bloke who'd offered us the weed had disappeared. I looked around the room packed with Irish gangsters and Rastas with attitude; the place was full of whores and suited crooks, wall to wall slime and debauchery. This was not the sort of place a good lad like me should be at all. I ordered a JD and coke at the bar from a woman that looked like she could crush Brazil nuts with her gold-encrusted fingers. Her hoop earrings were so heavy you could see little slitty holes that appeared in her lobes. She might have been pretty once in an operatic type of fashion, but her mouth was as rough as her language and her teeth were yellow and grey.

I scanned the room, the sort of scan that notices people but avoids eye contact at all costs. This was the sort of place you came to in bad movies and only when you were The Terminator. Wall to wall scum. I noticed Pat near the toilets having a proper heated discussion with the bloke who'd said he'd sort us out some weed. Things didn't look too smart at all; hands were being raised and Pat was looking aggressive to say the least. Occasionally I could hear raised voices as well; they were obviously exchanging anything but pleasantries.

Fuck: again the Rasta I'd hoped to avoid made eye contact with me and again gave the cut throat action. 'Blood clot,' he mouthed in my direction.

My bottle was well and truly going from vintage claret to white wine spritzer. I wanted to down my drink and bale out when Pat appeared and said, 'We're off, job done, sorted.' I necked my drink and made for the exit, relieved. I still made a show of walking to the exit in my best 'hard man with places to go' strut.

As we left the shit hole I asked Patrick, 'What was that all about and what's going on now?' Trying not to seem overly concerned or bothered, I added, 'Did you get the weed?'

As I spoke I noticed, a little way in front, the lad who'd led us into the den of ill repute in the first place. As we followed him I asked Pat again, 'What the fuck is going on?' He wasn't exactly being forthcoming and I wondered if he was still stewing from the row in the club; the conversation, though, was becoming a bit like a bad dream, a one-way conversation.

The more we walked around Soho's back streets, the more apparent it became that we were being joined by people connected to the weed man. The more corners we turned, the more clingers-on we seemed to be gathering. I knew Patrick was hard but at this stage there were about eight people following us. 'Seriously, Pat, what the fuck is going on and where the fuck are we going?'

'I'm going to get us our weed!' Pat snapped.

I guess I knew Patrick wasn't likely to be the type of bloke who would get skanked easily. I was well and truly far and beyond ready to call it a night and put it down to a lesson learnt and another experience had, but Patrick wasn't and one thing I'd never do is leave someone mid-flow like this. Someone once said these colours never run. Not my nan, though; she would have said kick them in the shins and walk away.

On we walked, single file into a dodgy, stinking multi-storey car park in the middle of Soho on the outskirts of the red light district. It was dark, very late and stank of piss. Yet on we went, Patrick and I following the weed dealer flanked by about eight of his mates. Shitting myself doesn't really do justice to the emotion. Accepting inevitability is more apt. Why the fuck was I there?

There was a hue of fuzzy orange light, soft buzzing and the sound of stale, stagnant water dripping. Did I fancy Pat and I fighting our way out of that situation? No. Over to you, God! I could only foresee my broken body left in tatters at the bottom of some crumby concrete stairwell. Autopilot was initiated: my brain had nothing left to give, and I was all out of ideas. If the moment arose and I could run, fuck would I run; if I had to fight, I'd fight to get myself clear and then run. In the meantime whilst I searched for better ideas I went back to God. 'You decide,' I muttered under my breath. Whatever happened I knew my mum wouldn't approve.

I decided the blokes looked like skinny tramps. Down we went to the basement of the squalid, damp, continuously dripping and piss-smelling car park in finest London Town. Sinatra never sang about this. The leader of the tramps we'd been following stopped by an air shaft; he reached above the vent and pulled out a concealed stash of smoking devices. The relief was instantaneous; I thought he was going to pull out a weapon. This fucker and his mates had come down here to smoke bongs. I thought it was a trifle extreme but hey, at least I wasn't going to die. This would be easy; I'd dealt with this sort of shit before, loads of times in fact. I'd almost happily indulge in a couple of toots and then get the fuck out of there; fuck the weed, they could keep it. At least it wasn't needles or glue.

Chief tramp boy's mates were clambering all over the show like fucked-up people-spiders all bringing out devices of their own and foil and shit. I decided in my head these guys were Soho's version of the cool kids who liked a smoke. Rather than sitting in cars down a country lane or round someone's house like I was used to they used the car parks. I supposed perhaps they might smoke more or less; I knew I'd soon find out.

The circle formed and the skinny fellows set to work preparing their tools for immediate use. I wasn't familiar with the foil joints but was ready for one and pass. They weren't finished; they obviously liked to pre-roll everything they had. All the while alert: occasionally a head would pop up like a mongoose listening to any noise. They certainly were a jumpy bunch.

'Pat, we get the weed and fuck off, yeah?'

No answer. He must still have been working on it, I supposed.

The first lad lit up and then the second and then everyone joined in. Christ, this was going to be a full on session of one and pass. A grey chemical cloud slowly engulfed our concave. The lad next to me passed me a joint. His mouth didn't look too skanky; some looked like they'd been having blow backs off car exhausts. His fingers were yellow and his hand shook momentarily as I took the joint.

Just as I took my first puff Patrick said, 'It ain't weed.'

I looked at him, holding his stare, and took a couple of tentative pulls. All seemed well; it certainly didn't smell or taste like skunk. For a fleeting moment I was worried and then as more came my way I started feeling pretty cool and quickly decided the skinnys weren't so bad either. I caught a few eyes and they almost seemed welcoming, like they were saying, 'Hello, mate, welcome to the group.'

'What the fuck is it, Pat?'

But Patrick had gone off on one and was preaching about how crack fucks you up and how long it took for him to get off it. The group seemed a little freaked out as he held court in the middle of their circle. He wasn't keeping his voice down and was clearly breaking all their rules. I could see his plan and it was working: they weren't in a fit state to bother him now he was playing with their heads and minds and they already wanted us to leave.

I didn't sleep for twenty-four hours and the urge to try to get some more lasted about the same time. Even the weed that Patrick had somehow managed to get at some point wouldn't put me to sleep. I decided then that crack wasn't for me.

28 – I COULD

My brain felt like it was leaking out of my ears so I slipped out of work at lunchtime to go to the gym across the road. It was either going to be that or throwing my computer and myself out of my third floor window. Why did it always seem to crash or start acting mental when I needed to use it the most? Then there was boring Glen who sat opposite me continuously on the phone just saying, 'Yes, yes, yes, yes, yes, err, yes, yes, yes, you know, err, yes, yes, yes, you know, err, err, yes, right, right, okey dokey, right, yes, yes, yes.' He wound me up with his selfish, whatever-you-have-done-I-have-done attitude. I felt like, rather than breathing calmly at my desk, I was panting like a dog.

I got to the gym and got ready. I put my iPod on and warmed up with a couple of rounds of skipping and now I was ready for a nice angry tune to punch the hell out of the heavy bag, imagining boring Glen and my bosses and the sultan and the doctors and everyone else who was in my head.

I could usually get hold of pretty much anything not normally available in chemists and hardware stores from Millwall Mike: Viagra, Class As through to tasers and possibly guns. Not that I'd necessarily wanted to, it's just nice to know sometimes you can get hold of anything should you really need it. Mike's extensive network of hoodlums and ragamuffins included mates of mates including Tommy the Van and Warren Peace. Chances were if Mike couldn't get something he knew someone who could, no questions asked.

I knew I'd have to be careful, though. If I ordered a piece of heavy-duty merchandise like a gun and didn't have a logical reason for wanting it they could and most likely would get twitchy. They were possibly too close as friends and contacts and if anything went tits up it wouldn't take Inspector Gadget very long to follow the crumbs. Not that I didn't trust them. No, I trusted them more than most of my best mates. But I'd still need to be discreet and if possible lie about my intentions as best I could to avoid raising any suspicions.

I'd also have the option of going further afield. I could always use mates of mates oop north; they wouldn't ask too many questions and the links would be far more stretched. It would probably mean bigger balls and another mission, but no doubt a week of chatting shit would have me in possession of any bits and bobs that I would need should I really need specifics,. Ex-football hooligans were good for that sort of thing.

29 – BOYS FROM BROS

'WHAT YOU DOING? You fucking prick, fuck off!'

I was simply running across the road. I was with the other lads from Moss Bros, the clothes shop where I worked, my first full-time job since leaving college. The pay was shit but it was a job. We'd had several beers after work in Charring Cross and were crossing the road towards Trafalgar Square en route to another pub in Covent Garden. No sooner had I put one foot on the curb, having jogged across the road because of the oncoming vehicles, than this bloke blatantly barred my path, pushing me back towards the traffic. I could have been hit by a car.

He pushed me again, probably, I thought, due to my language; more likely, in retrospect, because he was just looking for trouble.

Without further provocation I threw a perfect windmill style left, right, left, right, left, right, left, right combination. No punches seemed to connect with his face; he seemed to block or parry every punch I threw.

My momentum, however, had pushed him a little further away from me and afforded me a few seconds' respite. We stood facing each other like two dualists. My adrenalin hadn't even started pumping; all I felt was bemused and slightly bedraggled and out of breath. I straightened my jacket and tie; if nothing else I hoped I'd look good and my actions would serve as a warning not to be an arsehole in the future. Unfortunately he hadn't learnt his lesson at all. Worse still, he was just warming up, literally. He performed a mantra or whatever they call it in karate when someone does a series of rehearsed moves.

The bloke didn't look like the Karate Kid either; he was more or less the same age as me, much scruffier, though, and he had the slight look of a pikey about him with his old, worn Reebok tracksuit bottoms, longish greasy hair and pale complexion, and he was quite a bit taller than me, but most blokes are.

I looked round to find the lads I was with from work, and took a quick glimpse at them. I didn't want them to help me fight this bloke, I just wanted to be reassured they were witnessing the same thing as me. Their faces showed they felt as I did: a mixture of complete amusement and wonderment and a smidgen of utter bafflement. If I'd have been Indiana Jones or James Bond I would have simply shot him, but being me I just started to laugh. This pissed him off and Bruce Lee shuffled towards me. I had no choice but to remember the Queensbury rules and raise my guard in defence. I had a feeling he was going to kick me and I was feeling flat-footed compared to Mr-Bouncy-I-Know-Kung-Fu-Mother-Fucker. I decided if he tried to kick me I'd grab his leg and, and fuck...

WOO WOOO, flashing blue lights. The police arrived, skidding up next to us. Karate Kid legged it. I walked slowly into the road as the Old Bill clambered out of the car, demanding, 'Oi, you, what's going on here?'

I bent down, picking up my bag and walkman that had been half chucked loose into the road in the melee, and replied, 'He tried to nick my bag, Officer.' I pointed at the Karate Kid as he weaved through the crowd.

'Wait here!' they shouted and I said 'Okay', lying, as they ran off in hot pursuit of Mr Choppy.

I walked up to my colleagues and said, 'How about that beer then?'

30 – THEY SAY

I WAS SITTING STARING at all the cramped passengers on the Metropolitan line battling to get to work. I was lucky I got on earlier so I got a seat. I searched the carriage, ready to give my seat up to any pregnant ladies. I watched them all rocking and swaying in time with the train. Armpits in faces, everyone was standing in each other's space, all angrily rubbing themselves on each other, using free publications as a papery barrier or books, digital and paper versions, to hide their faces behind. One Asian looking girl had her music on so loud I tapped my feet along to her tunes. It seemed to annoy the old lady with a pointy nose and slithery lips who was doing her best to ruffle her paper and tut in the younger girl's general direction in the faint hope that her dagger looks would somehow result in her turning her music down. That wasn't going to happen; she was blocking the world out and I totally understood. I gave up reading about the latest nutter to go on a gun-shooting rampage through middle Britain. Why did they always go nuts in the rural suburbs? Why hadn't anyone gone on the rampage through London?

They say it's the quiet ones that you have to watch out for. I said that's bollocks. It's the ones that have taken the most shit that flip. It's not rocket science: leave a pot of water boiling on a hob and see what happens. Everyone has a limit; some people delay hitting it by seeking help from the bottle or diving head first into drugs or sex or gambling or violence. You have to really go for it to have a nervous breakdown unaided and without questionable vices. A nervous breakdown is your own natural, built-in fuse breaker, which physically hurts no one but yourself.

It's selfish people who say breakdowns affect the whole family and friends and everyone else as well as the person suffering the breakdown. I thought those people should try looking in the mirror. More than likely

71

one of the family or friends or the whole fucking family or all the so-called friends caused the problem in the first place. Breakdowns are selfish? Surely that's the whole fucking point.

If a saucepan of water is boiling over, only the person who put the pan on the heat can be blamed – you can't blame the water or the pan.

No one can't be broken; the strongest, hardest men on earth regularly prove it. Just look at the amount of boxers that are mentally wrecked, tortured by their own invincibility.

Generally a succession of events causes the volcano to erupt. Just how many people that get affected by the earthquakes and dust cloud's fallout remains to be decided by the grace of the gods!

31 – INTRUDERS

'THERE'S SOMEONE IN THE FLAT,' she whispered, entering my dreams.

'Go and see what they want,' I said, half asleep.

It was just another Friday night like many, many others: a few beers and then alcohol-induced slumber.

'Seriously! Please wake up. There's someone in the flat,' Carol pleaded.

I was wide awake now, the fear in her voice had smacked my senses alert and the noises sent shockwaves through my brain. This wasn't any other Friday night. I could feel my heckles rising. My ears strained to listen, my eyes searched shadows, my heart pumped adrenaline. I heard the creaking floorboards, doors banging, no silence, uninvited guests were in my house, there would be no reprieve, no bad dream.

I rolled forward and out of bed, picking up Excalibur, like Arthur with his sword only I had a baseball bat. I edged up to the bedroom door; with no time to think my hand reached out and lightly held the cold metal handle. I took one breath and turned the handle, pulling the door open, and started swinging with all my might. Crashing, doors banging, connections in the dark. Still I continued striking down with all my fear and fury, lashing out at shadows. I heard the lampshade smash and then footsteps stumbling in the night. I couldn't stop swinging the bat; panic drove me on.

I fumbled for the light in the hall; it still worked. The front door was hanging off its hinges, and I could still hear the intruders' murmurs on the other side; there was more than one for sure. I put my back to the door that was just clinging to the hinges by the top set, like a wobbly tooth, and pinned myself in the door frame. Bat in hand, one leg against the other wall, a human barricade. *I've got to keep them out*, I thought.

I grabbed the phone from the floor – the table it was sitting on was now in pieces – and phoned the police, sausage fingers and fuzzy head battling to remember simple functions. Nine, nine, nine…

'Police,' I said, not sure if I should keep my voice up or down. 'I want to report a break in.'

'Okay, sir, when did this happen?' the police call officer asked.

'It's happening now,' I replied.

'The intruders are still in the building, sir?'

'Errrr, yeah, they're on the other side of this door,' I said matter-of-factly.

'We're on our way, sir,' the call desk person replied.

'Good, good, quick as you can, please,' I said.

I hung up, listening to the continued banging around on the other side of the door. They were still here, very close. My pulse in my brain was almost as deafening in the quiet.

'The police are on their way,' I shouted, as much for the intruders' benefit as Carol's.

She gingerly looked around the corner at me, terror on her face and still naked, hugging a towel for protection.

'Could you please throw me some pants, please, thank you?'

I tried to put them on whilst still holding the baseball bat in one hand and the phone in the other; the cable got all tangled through my legs, goolies and pants. Only when I realised I didn't need to be holding the phone any more did I manage to untangle myself by putting the receiver back past my jacobs and through my pants.

'Fuck!' I could still hear them on the stairs outside the flat. My heart started pounding again as a fresh rush of adrenaline surged through my body. I braced myself again, unsure if they were coming back up the stairs or going down and leaving. My head was pounding like never before.

'Check the fucking flat,' I screamed at Carol; I couldn't hold the door and check. She was reluctant to move, petrified with terror. Thankfully it was only use on the inside. I heard more doors banging; the intruders were hopefully fleeing. I had to check they were gone.

I opened the front door, again swinging the bat into the gloom. I manoeuvred myself in a style reminiscent of American cops in the movies; that was the technique I had in my mind at least. Unfortunately I had a bat and would have definitely felt more comfortable holding a Glock 747 pump-action double-hard bastard gun. I edged tentatively down the dark flight of stairs; the flat next to mine had not been entered. I continued swinging at every corner.

A light switch: this would tell me if anyone was there and tell anyone who was there that I was coming. I hit the light, switching it on. No one was there. I edged forward a little quicker in the light. Next door, on another corridor, the hinge was broken. I swung the door open into more darkness, deafening creaking metal on metal quietly protesting in the evil silence, again sweeping the bat as hard as possible into the murkiness before stepping into its slipstream. There was another fumble in the blackness for the light switch, the sound of my breath like the ocean breaking on a pebbly beach. The light switched on, revealing another empty corridor.

There was more pace to my steps now, a determination to my stride. The next corridor was after the last of the three flats; the last flat looked undisturbed as well. It was sod's law! Given the choice of three apartments they had chosen mine, and whilst I was in bed as well. I wasn't sure who was more unlucky, me or them. The last door opened onto a T-junction, one way led to the right to an empty storage space behind a shop. This was a damp, gloomy, dark place at the best of times, without a light that I knew of as well. I pushed the door open, ignoring the darkened room, and headed straight for the front door exit. Part of me just wanted to run away up the road and into the night.

Flicking the final hall light on, I was sure they must have left the building unless they were hiding in the store room in the dark at the end of the corridor. I swung the front door open and felt the cool night air envelop me. I was then standing in the middle of a fairly busy street not that long after closing time outside a twenty-four-hour Tesco's holding a baseball bat and wearing nothing but boxer shorts. People didn't seem to care too much: most looked like they were keen to ignore me; others seemed to think I wasn't anything out of the ordinary. I scanned both directions, looking for anyone who looked like a wounded intruder. Nothing. I had hoped to see someone slumped in a doorway, battered and bruised.

I went back to the open front door, disappointed, and turned the light back on again; the damn thing had a thirty-second timer which always made me curse it. It was like it intentionally sped up whenever I needed more time. I waited for the thirty seconds to end and then I punched it again and ran into the space behind the shop. For a second I got paranoid and panicked, thinking they could have hidden in there and slipped back upstairs whilst I was outside in the street in my boxers. They could be upstairs now attacking Carol!

'Are you alright up there?' I called, trying to sound fine and in control, relieved that my voice still worked.

It was all clear upstairs and in the corridors and when the police turned up they told me to put down the bat.

32 – DOWN IN UPPER STREET

I WAS JUST STARING AT THE SELF-SERVICE TILL. I couldn't decide. Did I want cash back?

'Are you alright, sir?' the friendly M&S lady asked. She looked like a young, made-up Fatima Whitbread. I looked at her but couldn't answer her question.

'It's my entire fault, you see. I somehow persuaded her, God knows how or why, but I did.'

'Who did you persuade, sir? Is everything alright?'

I didn't know why I was speaking to her. All I'd come in for was a sandwich, a packet of crisps, a drink, a chocolate bar and some nuts. I clicked 'No' to the cash back and made my way out of the shop, still talking to the assistant, only this time in my head.

She'd never even wanted children, or so she said, and yet there she was. She hadn't really even begun to warm to the idea. I felt like she was doing it as the ultimate massive gift for me. I always complained I bought the best presents.

All I could do was say I'd support her no matter what she decided. I felt like I'd been in a similar situation before, only this time I was supposedly getting what I wanted. At the beginning I was as open to all the options as I could be, but as time wore on both of us knew I utterly preferred the idea of having a kid rather than an abortion, and slowly I think she did as well; she just hadn't accepted it yet, although I wasn't sure.

How much did I want a kid, though? Did I want it more than going out, more than going to West Ham or however many holidays to wherever in the world as we'd promised each other when we first met? To live comfortably was all Chloe wanted. Truth be told, I never really considered any of it before. The realisation that life would be the same struggle for us as it was for any family ate away at me. As weeks became months and still no decision was made, things slid until time ran out and the decision was made for us. For better or worse, we were going for it.

33 – SCARS

I HAD A SCAR ON THE BRIDGE of my nose from a messy night in Greenwich. We were all a little too high and had drunk far too much. I lived on the Isle of Dogs at the time with my mates Tom and Hayden, and we were ambling home after enjoying the usual pissed-up high jinks. I had jumped on Hayden's back, hoping for a lift home. He had decided to become a human hurricane instead and we'd both tumbled to the floor in different directions. I went face first into the curb and Hayden was flat out in the middle of the street.

As I rolled over, sniggering under the East End stars, an old lady walked past and gasped at the sight of me. 'Is he okay?' she asked, and everyone said that I was fine. 'Lawd help us,' were her parting words as Hayden got back to his feet. I felt alright; my wrist felt slightly sore but I guessed this was from breaking my fall as I swan-dived towards the deck. I was sure it would be fine in the morning.

Someone said if I had missed the floor I'd have discovered the art of flying but obviously I'd failed. I sat up, feeling a tickle on my top lip, like a fly or my nose was running. I pinched my nozzle, no snot, but I had blood on my fingers. The other lads, Bob, Ryan, Hayden and Tom, came over, laughing, and then stopped abruptly.

'What the fuck have you done to your face?' Bob asked.

'I don't know,' I said, thinking, *I can't see it.* 'Why?' I asked, already convinced by their faces that if I could see what they could see it wouldn't look pretty.

I'd split the top of my nose open and grazed my forehead and all down my cheek and even my chin.

Bob decided the best thing to do was check me in the light before making any rash decisions. As I walked the half mile further to my house blood trickled down my lips, causing me to huff and puff and spray fine droplets all over my already-claret-covered shirt. We weren't far from home but already I looked like I'd been shot in the head or had had my head run over. When we got in Bob took control of the situation and decided my hooter probably needed stitches. This was unanimously rejected as I'd spent the afternoon drinking and was also as high as a kite and no one at all fancied sitting in A&E with me tripping their socks off. So instead Bob went to work on my face armed with nothing but a few boxes of plasters.

When I woke up the next day, about Sunday lunchtime or midday to normal, everyday people, my belly acted as my alarm with a grumbling protest. I sprawled in bed, trying to piece together the night before and remember how I'd got home and into bed. I wasn't sure exactly but I knew something wasn't quite right. I rolled back the covers and my wrist felt like it was on fire. I tried to flex it but it was swollen to almost twice its normal size and totally lame. *Shit, that hurts*, I thought. But that wasn't all. I struggled out of bed and made my way to the mirror. My face felt unusually tight like someone had coved my face in glue overnight. I looked at my reflection and it was as bad as it could have looked without actually having lost an eye or an ear. I certainly looked like I'd been in a car crash and had gone straight through the window and then had the misfortune of the car driving back over my head before a herd of gazelles decided to trample me into the flora and fauna for good measure.

'What the fuck!' I shouted.

Bob had used a whole pack of plasters on my face to push the top of my nose back together. I had two black eyes, a bright red graze that was going to scab up absolutely fucking bloody lovely running the length of my face, and to top it all off my wrist was twice the size it usually was.

All of this wouldn't have seemed like such a big deal – and perhaps I seem a little vain in my reaction – but only a few days earlier I had accepted a new job and a day later I was due in my new position having only briefly met my colleagues. I looked at myself and contemplated what they would be seeing.

I turned up on the Monday morning with my arm in a sling, two black eyes and a face that looked like it had had a run in with a cheese grater. First impressions and all that!

I also had a scar on my belly I gained as a kid in Majorca on a hot, sticky, Mediterranean evening whilst on a family holiday. Like most little lads I liked to run around and jump up and down reaching for unreachable heights, super-charged on Coca Cola and E numbers. I was drawn like a moth to the flashing lights of the juke box. It had a glass front and although I could hardly reach the direction arrows that allowed you to choose your song I found by bouncing up and down I could just about hit the selector. This was until I found the slight chip in the glass that managed to open a nice slice on my belly. After lots of uncontrollable screaming, thinking my innards were going to fall out, a señorita from the hotel took control, deeming nail varnish was the best way to stop my guts from falling out, and finally put my mind to rest.

I had two scars on my left eyebrow, one going slightly uphill and the other going slightly downhill. The first came from rocking on a chair at my auntie's house: I went eyebrow first straight into a dinky toy on the kitchen table. The second came some years later when I was an adolescent on one of my last family holidays.

The thought of hedonistic parties, sleepovers, girls and getting drunk completely overpowered the interest in one- or two-week family holidays in sun or rain with Mum and Dad and sisters walking around boring touristy places in strange places like Wales or Sweden. On this occasion we were in Kos. I'd met a couple of younger Geordie lads who were keen on my middle little sister. They were nice lads and although they were a few years younger than me their parents deemed I was sensible enough and old enough to be allowed to take their little cherubs into town for a boy's night out. Somewhere along the line we ended up in some sort of bluesy rock and roll bar, and whilst dancing like idiots I was whacked around the head with a guitar. It didn't really hurt that much at the time, although my eyebrow was split open like a sliced tomato and I had the always pleasurable stare in the mirror and moment's realisation whilst blood streamed down my mush.

Then, as the sun rose and we made our way home, me with spilt eyebrow, one of the young Geordies with a massive love bite on his neck (unfortunately not from a girl either) and the other with a ripped-up shirt, we thought it would be a good idea to do a spot of skinny dippy. I dived into the swimming pool; that saved me needing to clean my face, clothes and war wounds.

Another childhood injury was my chipped incisor tooth. This distinguishing feature was gained whilst trying to break the land speed record for four boys going downhill on a garage-made go cart. This toboggan powered beast was created out of three large planks of wood, with the two heavy front wheels on one piece of heavy wood creating the front axle. This was steered by a thick piece of rope like the type we climbed at school. It also had a heavy-duty bucket seat, possibly for mentalists in cars, and finally another two heavy wheel-barrow wheels on the fixed rear axis. The cart measured about six feet in length and weighed more than any one lad could have possibly managed to drag around or stop on their own: it was definitely built for a team. It was created by Jack, Joe and Tony's dad. Being a complete nutter, he left off the brakes. The only way you could stop the beast was by jamming your feet on the floor, skidding until the soles of your feet burnt or, in times of extreme peril and desperate need, you could lock the front wheel into the central plank.

I broke my tooth when Peter, Joe and Tony and I were going full pelt and gained far, far too much speed. We were charging down Corona Road and momentum meant we weren't going to be stopping in a hurry or any time soon. At the bottom of the road was my house and usually we would have aimed to have stopped moving long before we hit my driveway as it was bordered with a cobbled brick curb that even in the luxury of a proper car with suspension you still needed to approach with care, let alone when you were approaching at great speed on a hard plank of wood jet propelled by hyper midgets with no suspension at all. We had all felt the pain of bumping over the bricks and the thought of getting whacked up the arse and propelled into the air, daylight between your arse and the planks of wood or even the uncomfortable chair, was enough to understand the need to use the emergency brake using the wheel jam technique. We were running out of road fast and had no choice; we might have even crashed straight into my house if we didn't stop soon. The soles of our feet didn't stand a chance at that sort of speed. We were burning it up.

Usually when utilising the front wheel jam technique you could expect quite a decent front wheel skid; however, this time somehow the wheel jammed against the cobbled stones, stopping us instantly, which resulted in us all doing a forward roll with the go kart pole vaulting from underneath us until the four of us lads lay face down in a heap on my drive and finally the vehicle landed on us. I was unlucky enough to have my face smashed into the street thanks to the massive wheel-barrow wheels, leaving me with the chipped tooth that you might have seen if I smiled.

34 – MANY HAPPY RETURNS

IT WAS MY BIRTHDAY. I was sitting with my grandad with tears flowing down my cheeks. I'd noticed his breathing change; I knew his six-week battle was coming to an end. He'd lost his ability to swallow when he'd had the stroke yet he still hadn't given up. He carried on fighting, occasionally smiling, constantly fidgeting, sometimes fitting, bruised and often muttering garbled messages of barely audible numbers. He acted out a strange sign language like he was trying to tell me something about cutting wrists or my wrists which I didn't understand. He didn't seem at all happy about his pants or his gowns like they were uncomfortable, and he didn't like getting injected or having his catheter or drips changed; I could see the angry humiliation in his eyes even if he couldn't voice his disapproval.

As I cried and warbled on about my problems, unloading my anger at work being shit, colleagues being arseholes, I'd even mentioned I might be becoming a father and he in turn would be a great-grandad, not that he wasn't already. He was just about the best man I'd ever known. I just thought in some way me having a child was relevant as he lay there with his life slipping away.

Suddenly he seemed not to be exhaling. I moved closer, holding his hand, telling him how much I loved him and that Nan was waiting for him and to not be scared and to go and find her for a dance. Then his breath stopped, he squeezed his eyes shut, his final bit of life drained away. The lights in the room flickered, the colour drained from his face and he was cold and gone. I couldn't stop looking at him; he seemed to keep changing colour, getting yellower and greyer. I didn't want to leave him. I couldn't stop looking at his hands. Grandad's hands had been there all my life guiding me; now they were lifeless and I felt lost and bitterly angry. Who would listen to me now? Whose opinions mattered to me like his?

After I couldn't cry any more I went outside and lit a cigarette. I couldn't think any more, my brain was totally numb. I fumbled in my pocket and pulled out my phone. It was on silent. I had missed several calls and had a few text messages. Without thinking I checked my voicemail mailbox. First message was from James saying, 'Wah hey, happy birthday, fucker, hope you have a good one, we'll go out soon and get messy, eh.' Second message was a client saying, 'Hello, just chasing my job. Can you call me as soon as possible and let me know where it is.' Third message, same client: 'Hello, we're still waiting for our job. We specifically asked for it to be delivered before half nine, it's now half ten and we haven't seen it. Because you haven't phoned we're none the wiser. I don't think this is a very good service at all so don't think we should be charged for this job. Phone me as soon as you get this message.' Fourth message: "Ello Pilot Light, just had the bloke from Gibbons Brady & Hartley on the phone chasing his job, stroppy fucker. Can you let him know it was delivered this morning at half nine and signed for by a Peter. Why are you late anyway? Get out of bed, you lazy bastard.'... 'You have no new messages.'

I couldn't bring myself to read my texts.

35 – VICTORIA LINE

CAROL AND I WERE ON THE VICTORIA LINE heading back to Finsbury Park. We had enjoyed a few pre-Christmas drinks in Covent Garden before heading up to Oxford Street on a mini, impromptu pub crawl. I was a little tipsy; we were both merry but definitely not pissed. We then headed home not particularly late, well oiled but in good spirits. We were happy. We weren't rich; we were young and had some aspirations. Her more than me, or her family had more for her than me; it didn't really matter – we were healthy and getting by. We were getting on well. Past troubles were literally that: past troubles.

We giggled as the tube train bounced us around on our seats. I hadn't really taken much notice of the other passengers; I was in my own little bubble with Carol. The guy sitting in front of me was Oriental looking but seemed a happy enough chap; so much so that when I took out a packet of square, salty flavoured crisps from my bag, after offering some to Carol, I also offered them to him. Carol laughed; he nodded, smiled and said, 'No, thank you.' An older lady, weathered by London living, looking perhaps ten or twenty years older than she really was, adorned in a heavy, woven, thick-checked, greeny-brown coat that could have come straight out of Nora Batty's wardrobe, clutched her purple, fake leather handbag with bright gold-plated buckles closer to herself; she seemed to think for a second about giving me a dirty, disapproving look before relenting and breaking into a little grey-toothed smile. It was as if she said 'No, thank you', just in case I offered her a crisp as well. I imagined they would play havoc with her teeth.

We were having fun nonetheless, and so many journeys on the underground are so utterly insular and devoid of any feeling or actions or human interactions. We were having fun and didn't really care about anyone else.

I realised I hadn't offered any crisps to the guy sitting beside me on my left. He was listening to his walkman. The first time I offered him a crisp he didn't seem to notice me or was deliberately ignoring me. I offered him a crisp again and this time he turned to look straight at me. I waved the crisps at him and mouthed, 'Do you want one?'

He didn't say a word, he just looked at me for a moment. He stared straight through me. He reminded me of the actor Tim Roth. I asked again, 'Do you want a crisp?' He blinked, took out his earphones and leant down between his legs to retrieve a rucksack sitting on the floor. I thought he might have a packet of crisps himself as he put his headphones into his bag, which he placed back on the floor. He then turned to face me, but in his hand he held a Stanley knife no more than five or six inches from my face. My eyes flicked between the blade and his eyes and mouth. He started talking monosyllabically. I was aware of all the other passengers including Carol recoiling, trying to put distance, any distance, between me and him and them. My heart pounded; time slowed down. Every miniscule movement of the blade was tracked by my eyes. I was supremely calm but utterly attentive.

'Are you taking the piss out of me?' he asked coldly.

'No,' I said, staring at the blade.

'Because if you were I would fucking cut you up,' he said.

'I only offered you a square crisp,' I said, trying to open negotiations. I was trying to persuade myself that if he was going to cut me up he would have done it by now, and whilst I concentrated on his hand, which took on the look of a rattle snake all coiled up and ready to strike, I started thinking about grabbing his hand and fighting him back. Would any other passengers get involved? The way they had edged away suggested to me I was on my own.

He was still talking to me; he was quite calm but definitely unhinged. He wasn't going to let the situation fizzle out. He was still questioning why I had offered him a crisp, thinking I had an ulterior motive or was in some way taking the piss out of him. I noticed he was gradually moving off his seat, trying to stand up, or at least he wanted to be standing up. So, keeping my distance and concentration on the blade, I gradually stood up as well. We were roughly the same size. My peripheral vision was totally aware and focused on his whole body, but the blade was the focal point.

Everything I said he seemed to ignore or repeat. He seemed lost as to what he was supposed to do next.

'Look, mate...' I said.

'I don't 'av to look at anything,' he murmured back.

'I'm sorry!'

'You aren't sorry!'

'All I did was offer you a crisp!'

'Why would I want a crisp from you?'

'You wouldn't necessarily want a crisp from me!'

'I didn't want anything from you!'

'I know now and I'm sorry you didn't want one.'

'You aren't sorry; you were taking the piss.'

'How was me offering you a crisp fucking taking the piss?'

'Don't you fucking swear at me!'

'I think you're overreacting, mate.'

'I ain't your mate and I think you're taking the piss.'

'Put the knife away, mate.'

'Fuck you, I told you I ain't your mate. Fucking make me put the knife away.'

'Look, mate, I said I'm sorry. Let's just forget it, yeah?'

'I won't forget it and nor should you.'

'Come on, mate, this is stupid.'

'Don't call me stupid.'

'I wasn't calling you stupid.'

The situation wasn't improving, and with us both now standing and swaying with the train the conversation was leading to a climax: we were either going to end up in a fight or the train was going to arrive at the next station and things would come to a head. I had no idea what the outcome would be. I had tried to keep my distance, and getting close enough to head-butt him would have put me within slicing reach. I could hear Carol moving behind me. I wasn't sure if she was getting out of the way or going to intervene using some feminine charm.

I continued watching the blade, not so worried about the damage one swipe would cause. I was vain but not so vain that I was petrified of getting cut up. But I was on a train with normal people who were unquestionably scared. I had caused this. The guy hadn't wanted a square crisp and certainly didn't want to back down. Could I knock him out with one punch? It didn't feel likely. I could grab his knife hand and hope and pray for some intervention. Why hadn't I acted straight away? How had I let the situation build to this? What was the right thing to do? Negotiations had got me nowhere.

Then the leather wall appeared. Out of nowhere it seemed to me. Certainly from somewhere behind me a man mountain wearing a long black leather jacket appeared between me and the guy with the blade and gently but forcefully bore down on my aggressor using nothing but his huge size as intimidation. The guy with the knife backed away until he was forced to sit down. I couldn't hear anything being said. I just backed away into the aisle and towards the door, ready to jump off the train at the next stop. Would the big guy be okay? Should I stay and make sure he was okay as well? Carol grabbed me by the hand. I looked at her and she was ashen and wide eyed. Looking back around the train carriage I saw the older Chinese looking man and the old lady still clinging to her handbag didn't look much better. I'd ruined their journey; her eyes simmered with resentment.

I didn't know who the leather wall was; I guess he could have been my guardian angel. Or hell's angel? I never figured my angel would be a man much taller than six foot and sporting an early eighties-style mullet and wearing a long leather coat.

36 – COLD PILLOWS

MY BED WAS COLD, and it didn't feel clean like it used to; I probably should have changed the sheets by now. That wasn't my forte. I was drunk and tearful. I wasn't sure what time it was. I wanted to go back to sleep. I wanted to carry on the dream. The street lights were shining through the blinds so it was either early or late. *Perhaps I should have another whiskey to put me back to sleep*, I thought. I tried to think happy thoughts to start a nice dream off. My body ached and itched and I couldn't get comfortable. One pillow wasn't enough and two felt like I was sitting up straight. Chloe would have snapped at me by now.

I know what I should have said:

'My wife, my soul mate, you are the only real love of my life. I have loved you from the very first moment I saw you. I'll never forget my interview with The Printing Company. As I passed the office you were simply getting on with your work in your tight red trousers, flirting with the guys just by being you, perfect, all bubbly and beautiful. I was determined to get the job so I could work with you, just to be with you, to get to know you.

'These gifts I will get are for you, for us. I promised we would live happily ever after and we would get there in the end. I know things haven't been easy and I have been a twat, but thank you for sticking with me. I know I said it didn't matter if we didn't have any children and I honestly meant it. I always wanted you over anything and everything. All I ever wanted was you. You always said we don't know what's around the corner and let's see how things turn out; well, I'm going to make things turn out alright.

'We will be rich; we will be able to live comfortably. You don't have to worry. I love you, sweetheart. We will have the lovely house and the life you always wanted. We will be secure.'

37 – HOGMANAY

I'D APPOINTED MYSELF to the role of social secretary. I'd found the club night, sorted the tickets, filled the flat with booze. The likely crew were all assembling and on their way from all over the country. Everyone was due at mine first and then off to the club we'd go. New Year's Eve was sorted; I'd planned it all perfectly and all that was left to do was go and enjoy.

The flat was full with people, everyone nattering, even my budgie. Pre-club excitement washed down with vodka and Red Bull. My mates and mates of mates were all looking forward to the night ahead. Some people, however, had opted to go straight to the club; initial worries about traffic jams caused last minute changes of plan.

Still the crowd and general mood deemed the best course of action would be to get as drunk as possible on my cheap supplies at home before heading to the club that was more than likely going to be charging over the odds as usual on NYE.

I began to feel my feet itching as time went by and felt the crowd needed encouragement to drink up and party on. This was probably a bad decision. I drank my drink and it was quickly replaced with another that was supposedly mine as well. I encouraged everyone to follow suit. No joy.

I didn't want the guys who were going directly to the club to have to wait around all night whilst these piss artists fannied around getting merry on my supplies. I decided to neck a few more unattended glasses. I believed this was the best way to get everyone out of the flat and on their way as quickly as possible. I necked a couple more; only these didn't taste the same: no Red Bull, just vodka. Still, my plan was working.

'Come on, you fuckers, let's go!'

The added urgency to my voice and the volume of booze I'd drunk had begun to have the desired effect. Those who still guarded their drinks frigidly finished what they had begun and stubbed out fags and joints, then put on jackets and finally began making their way downstairs.

'Woo hooo, we're finally off,' I said, looking at Carol who was still entrenched in a conversation with her mates and not looking like she was interested in leaving.

We descended the three flights of stairs, noisy and expectant. The words from the tune 'Tonight it's part time, it's party time tonight, squeeze my tits' rang in my ears; the last song we'd heard on the CD player before leaving. I grinned at the motley crew gathered outside as I slammed the front door shut.

'Do you want to give us our tickets now?' Farrah, one of Liam's mates, asked.

I checked my pockets, shit! That was lucky; we'd nearly travelled all the way to the club without realising I'd left the tickets upstairs in the flat.

'Well remembered,' I said. 'I'd better go back upstairs and grab them.' I saw a few faces looking at me, thinking *Idiot*. I patted down my pockets in disbelief that I could have forgotten the keys as well. 'Fuck, I must have left them upstairs as well. Carol, can I use your keys?' *Please say you have yours*, I thought.

'No, I haven't brought a bag.'

'Fuck.'

Mates who'd previously been undecided were rapidly coming to the conclusion that I was a bit of a tool; and a prize one at that.

'What are you going to do now?' James asked whilst Carol looked at me like I was a piece of shit on her shoe. This was now becoming the general theme of the group's conversation and everyone was chipping in: 'Yeah, what are *you* going to do now?'

'Fuck a duck a day,' was all I could say. I had to use my last few functioning brain cells in a hurry and hoped they weren't as fucked as I felt; I was rapidly going from hero to zero. Big Tam and Farrah and a few other lads were recommending kicking the doors down to get to the flat. My problem with that was the three new communal doors in between the road and my abode! Not an option.

'The pub,' I announced. Everyone groaned; they didn't want to spend NYE in a pub.

'Not for a beer,' I hastened to add. I thought it was a great place to ask for a ladder. I lived on the middle floor and if I could get onto the flat roof I'd be able to open the window to the lounge and grab the tickets and keys and we were sorted. All I'd need to do was to get onto the roof. Hey presto, well done brain cells. I ran up to the local Wetherspoon's about five doors up and explained my dilemma. The old battleaxe took pity on me straight away and to my surprise sent me round the side of the pub where a ladder was waiting for me.

I made my way back to the flat feeling prematurely triumphant. No way would they expect me to return with a ladder. I hoped the group would be with me; these sort of hurdles pop up and make some groups of people grow together and enjoy the challenge, but at the moment I felt like the person who was ruining everyone's lives. *Fuck it.* I set the ladder and climbed the steps. Unfortunately for me, even with my arms and fingers fully extended I was still a good foot short. I went back down the ladder, searching for reassurances and reinforcements – even someone a foot taller would have easily reached. None were forthcoming. 'What the fuck!' No one said a word; they just left me with the dilemma.

I went back up the ladder, thinking one big jump up, a firm grip and I should be able to pull myself up, should, should, should... 'Could someone at least hold the ladder for me?' It was the least they could do I decided.

One, two, three, *fuck it.* I jumped up, feeling the ladder shift a little. *Cheers for the support.* I managed to catch one hand on the flat roof, which was a good thirty feet up in the air. As my momentum and equilibrium righted itself and my clambering free hand fell drastically short, my other hand held for a millisecond and then I felt the gravel under my fingertips begin to slide. Finally I let go as if the inevitable fall was more expected than the successful climb. I fell down horizontally amongst the crowd of my so-called friends and loved ones. My left wrist and head took most of the impact.

I lay still for a second, defeated and broken. I could hear them sniggering at me. Humiliated, I reacted the only way I knew how. With all my remaining power, I shot up and ran off as fast as I could. I made it across the crossroads, running full pelt in between the lights, then something strange happened. The path I was running along seemed to rise up at a peculiar camber, pushing me straight into a shop door. I whacked my head again, and lost consciousness.

As I drifted in and out I saw myself being thrown over someone's shoulder. I guessed it must have been Big Tam, Liam's mate. I was upside down in a fireman's carry. This was a strange way to go clubbing, but as long as we got there needs must, I supposed. In between opening and closing my eyes I put my hand in sick down his back; surely he couldn't go out like that. There was crashing and banging as doors were kicked in.

I was then on the carpet being manhandled into the recovery position. I could hear my sister saying I had pissed everywhere.

I came round in hospital mid conversation. I was chatting with the doctor who was examining my swollen limp wrist like a scene out of a pet program where an otter has got its paw trapped in a coke can or something and the vet is talking to the wounded animal like it understands English.

'And if I do that does it hurt?' said the doctor.

'Err, yes, please don't do it again. Why am I sitting here wearing my long, grey winter coat, boxer shorts and big old clumpy boots? I'd never go clubbing in this outfit.' Either it had been a really good night and I was seriously off my pickle or something was awry.

'I've got to go, Doc, I'm going to be late. I've organised everything. Thanks for your help, see you later.'

I got up and ran out of the hospital. I was sure I was dreaming or tripping. My head was banging and the lump on my forehead was testament to it. My arm was in a sling and bandaged up. I really was only wearing boxers and my long grey winter coat and was supposed to be going clubbing! 'What the fuck is going on? Where am I and where is everyone? Am I sleepwalking? Is this a nightmare?' I was chatting to myself, hoping to find some answers.

I needed a cab and fast and saw one straight away as I left the hospital. I ran towards it waving like an escaped mentalist. I had no idea where I was. Carol called out from behind me and ran up, joining me as I clambered into the cab.

I didn't say a word as she explained that the others had kicked the doors in on the flat, they'd struggled to put me into the recovery position, they'd called an ambulance and they'd then sent me to hospital. Some of the group, including my sister Sam, had stayed at the flat. They'd called an emergency locksmith, but unfortunately a whole new door would be needed. I'd pissed myself, attacked the ambulance staff and told them I'd been doing heroin. I'd puked on someone's back and generally been a complete nightmare.

I wasn't going to be going clubbing, I'd missed the start of the New Year and no one would be celebrating. I felt the tears roll down my cheeks as utter dejection ran riot. It wasn't my fault. It wasn't my fault.

When I got home some of the guys and girls had returned from clubbing and joined up with the ones who hadn't bothered going out at all. Everyone was in a mood with me. James told me I'd ruined everyone's night and they wanted me to know. I thought I could hold my hands up and take responsibility for getting pissed, that was true, but couldn't help feeling someone else could have organised the tickets and someone else should have had their keys and someone else taller could have reached the roof and everyone could have got a wriggle on and left the flat when I was ready. I had paid literally for everything.

38 – I'VE DONE

As I PUT ON MY BLACK TIE, looking at my reflection in the mirror, I recognise the man in front of me but he looks different, naked although dressed. Another tear rolls down my cheek although the feeling of pain doesn't exist. I just feel alone.

I've done the London marathon, I've ridden from London to Brighton, I've walked on glaciers in Iceland and volcanoes in Hawaii, I've ice-canoed down rapids, I've climbed mountains, I've done mushrooms in Bali and Thailand, I've won handwriting competitions and beanbag races at school, I've graduated from college, I've loved and lost and loved again more than once, I've been sacked, I've broken a world record, I've been on television, radio and in the newspapers, I've swam with turtles and barracudas, I've walked with sharks swimming around my ankles, I've shot guns, I've driven in fast cars, I've been high, I've been low, I've been to West Ham vs Millwall several times, I've seen leopards in the wild, I've seen dolphins, I've flown in a helicopter and small propeller planes and small and big jets, I've seen the Queen and Nelson Mandela, I've seen Madonna, INXS and Oasis perform at the old Wembley and I've seen shit at the new one, I've been in a band, I've been skiing but preferred snowboarding, I've played the clarinet and bongos and had a drum kit, I've had sex on a train, I've beaten all my friends at darts and pool.

And none of it matters.

39 – BOB MARLEY

I WAS IN BALI FOR TWO REASONS: the first was to check on the mental state of my sister who was midway through travelling the world and causing the family some understandable concern; and the second reason was to propose to Carol in what had become a kill or cure solution I'd deemed totally unavoidable and unfortunately necessary. I had travelled with a ring; I'd decided to wait for a starry night, buy a bottle of champagne and do the deed, no doubt ruining my life in the process.

In addition to my girlfriend Carol, our travel party included my other sister Claire, my sister's gay boyfriend Paul and his newly acquired Balinese travel companion Cody. That made three girls, two gayers and me.

Clubbing was fun when we eventually got there, but getting anywhere took forever because we'd need to do a fashion show each night before going out. I even found myself making an effort and being bothered if no one commented on my outfits. We spent most days on the beach or exploring islands. Sometimes we'd go our own way just to meet up in the evening and then go and get drunk and have a disco.

As we sat around in the cafe having met up to discuss the evening plans we ordered a round of special 'Bong Lasses', or Mushroom Shakes as they're better known. We had all eaten and felt it would be a fun way to spend the evening. Nothing ventured nothing gained was the general consensus. Everyone felt fine sitting in the cafe: the cooling sea breeze, ambient music in the background, other people's voices laughing and happy; no problems at all.

'Who wants to have a paddle?' Paul said, looking longingly at the sea.

The girls all loved the idea so we paid the bill and left the cafe, headed over the dusty road and meandered down the empty idyllic beach to some abandoned plastic chairs stranded on the sand. Carol was looking very pale; we walked her to the chairs with calm words of concern and sat her down. Her eyes closed and she seemed to lose consciousness. We fanned her with our hands and asked if she'd like some water. No reply.

'Come on, Carol, wake up.' We were all getting a little nervous. The term 'throwing a whitey' couldn't have been more appropriate. Massaging hands and chit-chatting worriedly overcame the group; this was a massive downer just when everyone was beginning to feel funky.

'Perhaps we should find some help?' my sister Claire suggested.

'What can we say?' I shot back. 'Oh, we've all just taken mushrooms!'

I was acutely aware we were shortly going to become a bunch of gibbering idiots and I wasn't sure how well that would go down with the local authorities. And besides, I was sure she would be fine; everyone was just panicking. Two girls and two gays had that effect; it was time for me to take control. I was the alpha male, at least I hoped I was.

'Listen to me, Carol; wake up now otherwise I'm going to pour this cold bottle of water over your head!'

Her body shuddered! A reaction. Her eyelids flickered.

'Come on, Carol, wake up, please,' I urged, believing my harsh tactics were working but needing immediate results otherwise the pink army would take control and God knows where that would lead. At one point on my sister Sam's travels she had ended up measuring Paul's head with a tape measure so paranoid had he become that his brain was expanding.

'Can you hear me? I've got the water and I'm going to pour it on your head now. Three, two...'

On the count of one she convulsed from her feet up to her head like a body popping caterpillar. Everyone gave her space. Her eyes opened with a fixed stare straight ahead, her feet shot up and down and her waist followed and finally her back and shoulders flung her head forward like she'd been sitting in an invisible bumper car. Then she shot projectile vomit out into the sand.

We stood around watching her, momentarily flabbergasted. I was sure I'd seen her shake a devil from her body. As the girls rubbed her back, wiping tears from her eyes, a visibly shaken Paul, leader of the pink army, exclaimed, 'Millions and millions of cockroaches!'

'What on earth are you talking about, Paul?' I asked.

'Millions of cockroaches just poured out of her mouth!'

Bloody hell! I thought she'd expelled a demon and Paul had seen cockroaches pour out of her mouth. Perhaps a marriage proposal was a bad idea for other reasons too.

I couldn't stand it any longer on the beach; everyone was nattering nonsense.

'Who wants a drink?'

Everyone looked at me like I'd gone stark raving mental. Perhaps all they saw and heard was me barking and looking like a little purple fluffy dog; it was entirely possible.

'Listen, I'm going to get a JD and a bottle of water. Does anyone want anything?' Nobody wanted to leave the beach or the familiarity of the shared nonsense. I was partly relieved, and also hoped they would all stick together and stay where they were rather than wandering off chatting gobbledegook.

I set off for the bar. The sand felt about two feet deep and every footstep was a massive effort. I was worried if I stopped I might sink out of sight. I crossed a bouncy castle sandy road as quickly as possible, looking around me in case any vehicles or bikes or even people were coming, and made my way up to the biggest wooden staircase I'd ever seen. It was like whole oak trees or perhaps sycamore had been chopped down and placed on top of each other to make the giant wooden steps. When I got to the top I was knackered and didn't want to turn around for fear that I'd be above the clouds. I'd risked a quick glimpse on the way up but everything was fucked: I'd seen two red suns and a light beam shooting straight for me. I blinked a few times and made my way towards the dark club. A gorilla and the Grim Reaper were standing by the door but I didn't want to chat.

As I entered I could hear banging house music and cheers and shouting coming from the back. I headed straight for the bright light of the bar and ordered two JD and cokes and a bottle of water from a girl who looked like a baby and then about four years old. I looked away before she changed again. 'Thank you,' I said without knowing if I'd actually paid and if I had whether I was waiting for any change. I thought it would be a good idea to dunk my head in the sink in the loos to see if it might freshen me up a little. Perhaps I might even squeeze out a wee. I was enjoying my little adventure and was happy with the way I was holding it together. I made my way to the toilet with the bottle of water in my trouser pocket, weaving through a melee of people, concentrating on not spilling the JDs. I couldn't help noticing the crescendo in the cheering.

I stumbled on regardless; the toilet was in the corner of the darkened room, highlighted by a luminous picture of a little boy pissing like a fountain. I bundled past men in Irish rugby tops and pirouetted past flip flops, smelt suntan lotion and heard Balinese, Australian and British accents all laughing and shouting in a cacophony of voices. I noticed the dartboard on my way to the toilet; it looked like it had one dart protruding and then became a kaleidoscope and then a spinning roulette table and then a dartboard again only now there were two darts sticking out of it. I heard more shouting and made my way into the toilet.

When inside I wanted to splash my face with water but I'd need to be careful and refuse to look at myself in the broken mirror. If the water looked green it was sure to be battery acid and no doubt its effect would warp my face. I pottered around for a while like an old man searching for somewhere to put my drinks whilst I went for a wee. There was no space anywhere so I put them in the sink. I was a little worried I'd been in the toilet for hours and not sure where or whether I'd actually been for a piss already so I left the toilet and heading back towards the cheering.

My eyes couldn't cope with the change from the bright light of the bathroom to the darkness of the club and I was tempted to go back to the light of the loo whilst my head adjusted to the slight headache and strain from trying to focus my eyes in the dark. As I bumbled towards the exit some burly bloke who looked like Fred Flintstone stopped me and shouted over the music.

'Mate, you dammed loon, you know you walked through the middle of a darts game, right?'

I didn't say a word.

'You oughta be more careful, cobber!'

I couldn't fathom what he was talking about or what on earth he meant so I told him not to worry.

'I'm sure it will all work out fine in the end,' I reassured him. I figured he must be disillusioned or something; I understood his pain.

I made it out of the club and found the others on the beach. The fire in the sky had gone. Sam had gone to the loo in the bar but everyone else seemed to be keeping it and themselves relatively together. Even Carol had colour back in her cheeks, whilst the gays were happy still chatting shit. Claire took some JD from me and said she ought to check on Sam, who'd been gone almost as long as me.

When they returned Sam was looking really awkward and wanted to head home. We set off in triangle formation, me at the front, two girls behind and Sam and the two gays bringing up the rear. As I turned round to check I noticed Sam looking uncomfortable more than once, she kept pulling her knickers out of her bum and was walking funny. I was getting worried something bad had happened in the loo. Thankfully after a brief chat she revealed she had had a problem staying on the toilet seat. Sitting on the floor, or rather sliding around on a floor, in the nicest of bogs is a pretty grim thought, but in a club in a seedy Balinese crapper! Absolutely gross! She said she had spent ages trying to clean herself up. I remembered then promising I'd check up on her well-being. 'Yeah, Mum, she's coping really well, but not being able to sit on a toilet seat without falling off might be a bit of a problem.'

We all felt it would be a good idea to return to the rooms to freshen up and ride out the storm for a while, at least until we felt capable of normal behaviour in any bars and clubs. I felt it was quite possible we could all completely lose it on the beach under the gaze of the tourist-filled cafes, watching the sunset over the Indonesian sea.

We walked on in our silent triangle formation; at least I was silent, but my brain was playing tricks already and I was intent on keeping it real for as long as necessary. I wouldn't propose tonight but at least I could put on a nice outfit.

40 – RUBY

Sitting in the local curry house, I was convinced they had forgotten my order. I downed my complementary cocktail and ordered a Singa beer to wash it away. I also asked for a pen and paper so I could start writing a list.

Car – buy off eBay
Folding bike – get from one of the lads
Satchels and bags for bike – cycle factory
Plastic disposable bags – Robert Dyas, B&Q, Wickes
Family-size disposable BBQs – Poores or Budgens
Branch Cutter – B&Q, Wickes or Garden Warehouse
Wet wipes, cleaning products and rags – cash and carry
Taser – Millwall Mike
Good quality waterproof, lightweight black coat – Timberland or fishing shop
Large portfolio – The Art Shop
Stanley knife – B&Q
Fishing tackle and maggots.
Drugs.

41 – TATTOO

I FELT LIKE I HAD LOST EVERYTHING. I'd certainly lost Carol, my job and my house. It was only a matter of time before my marbles followed. I knew I could get back on my feet, I knew the pain of breaking up with someone, especially when it was that messy, was going to be a long and painful process, but given time I would mend.

Things had come to a head after I checked her phone messages. I knew it was snooping but I was sure something was going on. She had obviously been with someone else and I felt sick, angry, hurt and dirty. I threw the phone at her, leaving a hole in the bathroom door, and then she was gone.

Work was a pain. It was a new job, but trying to come to terms with a messy break to a long-term relationship and starting a southern sales office for a company based in Newcastle just wasn't happening. Really all they wanted from me was my database. I felt used by my ex, and was being used by my new employers. Within a month of moving into a new house I was also looking for a new job and had split up with my fiancée.

We had moved into the flat in Archway about two weeks before we split up. We had signed a rolling six month contract. So I was stuck in a flat not particular near any friends, out of work and clean out of love, and with no way of knowing how I was going to pay the rent.

I was twisted with anger and jealousy. I could have ripped myself into tiny chunks. I would have cried had I not been so angry. What way do you turn when you feel utterly humiliated in everything you've done? I felt like I should have screamed but I would have messed that up as well.

I woke up from a particularly heavy JD session. I hadn't changed. She'd said 'You've changed', but how had I changed? I hadn't, that was the problem. She had tried to change me and it hadn't happened. I wasn't going to change.

So I understood, I was right, I couldn't ever forget. I mustn't ever let myself be put in that position again. I had to find away to protect myself in the future. As my mate Mick used to say, 'You have to stand up for what you once stood for.' What did I stand for? Absolutely nothing! But that didn't change the fact that I couldn't forget who I was and the fact that she had tried to change whoever I was. I had to act now. There was only one thing for it: I'd get a tattoo, that way I'd never forget, that way I'd be constantly reminded of who I really was and what I stood for. I'd get my own name tattooed on my arm.

I had signed or tagged my way through school, art college and several jobs in various permanent structures in and around Essex and London. My tag was well rehearsed, so after a couple more JDs I set off with my hand-drawn artwork, my signature, and headed for Aladdin's Cave on Holloway Road.

I walked without any nervous anticipation; I wasn't worried at all. It was fate and I had to do this. I passed the yellow building, looking at the pictures of Maori patterns and tribal decorations and other inspirational bits of artwork.

I pushed open the door and entered. A large punk was sitting in a dentist's chair. I could hear the electric drill as well. The punk didn't turn around, which I thought was strange and a little rude, but from behind his massive, spiky, tattooed head had the air of 'fuck off' and 'I don't give a fuck' written all over it, so I thought I'd best be polite and patient.

'Be with you in a minute, mate,' I heard a voice say that appeared to resonate from the punk, so I said, 'No worries, mate.'

I couldn't hear much over the compressors and the dentist drill noises, and as I could only see the punk I figured it was him I was conversing with. That's when the punk swivelled slightly and revealed the tattoo artist between his legs. As the massive old punk stood up and pulled on his camouflage army trousers I was temporally unsure whether the tattoo artist was plying his trade by administering some sort of oral pleasures. I wasn't sure what made me feel more uneasy: the thought of the two of them sharing a sexual moment or the punk having his groin area tattooed. 'Clean needles, please!'

Aladdin gestured for me to take a seat whilst he dealt with the spiky haired fella and put away his drawing tools. I sat in a hungover daze with my scrap of paper with my hastily drawn tag, staring at an aquarium full of deformed goldfish. Shubumbkins or something; one was trying to suck another one's eye off. I was lost for a moment in their battle, gripped, worried sick about the little fella's eye. *Swim away, little fella, don't let him suck off your eye!* I wondered what the fish made of the outside world that they saw. Probably not much, I decided.

One fish would say, 'Look at that big fella getting a tattoo. Whoa, he's getting his groin tattooed!'

And another one would say, 'What did you say, Goldie?'

'Oh, it doesn't matter. What have you been up to?'

'Oh, you know, not much. Bit of swimming. You?'

'Not much, the same really, swimming, shitting and eating food that tastes like flies. Have you seen that big fella over there? What's he doing?'

'Looks like he's getting his... Whoa! Oh my God, did you see that?'

'See what?'

'Err, I don't know.'

'Me neither.'

'What you been up to?'

'Oh you know… this and that...'

'Excuse me, mate, wakey wakey. Can I 'av your artwork, please, sunshine?'

I was snapped out of my fishy drama and passed the tattoo artist my drawing.

'Is it a Chinese symbol?' he asked.

'No, it fucking isn't,' I replied a little more testily than needed, thinking, *It's a sign of life's dramas paradoxically symbolised in the battle between good and bad; it's a reflection of all that's wrong in the world; it's a hyper junction leading to a port hole where everything makes sense; it's an ancient saying reflecting good overcoming bad; it's, it's...* 'Well, actually, it's my name, but it does look quite like a Chinese symbol I suppose,'

42 – JOURNEY BEGINS – SATURDAY, 11AM TO SUNDAY 2AM

I'D FOLLOWED THE NORMAL FOOTBALL Saturday routine: woken up as usual with a stinking hangover and made my way to London listening to my iPod, avoiding people everywhere at every junction, determined to become just another person looking and smelling a bit rough on the train, subtly blending into the background. I met the lads at The Black Lion in Plaistow; it was the same old eventful game against Bolton, a grey sodden day both mild and drizzly, just like the football. I drank through my hangover only to have another one kick in by half-time. West Ham weren't going to be lifting my spirits today. After a few more drinks following the game I said my goodbyes and made my way back to the West End alone.

I stopped off at a club called Movida near Oxford Street. I'd been there with Chloe a few years earlier. I'd gone that Saturday after West Ham as well and was drunk, but because I with her they let me in; they didn't let me in this time, though. I looked like a pissed-up, underdressed football wrongun, and they had some high class rollers pulling up... one of whom I recognised: it was the sultan of wherever with his harem. I milled about for a bit but, feeling angry and with nobody to phone to say I'd be home at whatever time, I got the fast train from Euston to get home as quickly as possible. Again I drifted off, lost in my iPod. I listened to 'The Rat' by The Walkmen several times, feeling anger burn away inside me. Just when I was ready to hit something or cry I switched to 'Sabotage' by the Beastie Boys and felt instantly alive again.

When I got home I picked up the car keys and drove over to Chloe's parents. They were away in Sarasota, America as they needed a break. I didn't blame them. I had a set of keys just in case I fancied doing some fishing on the canal behind their house. I turned off the burglar alarm and took some bits out of the car and put them on the boat out the back. I put the keys in the boat and locked the house up and was ready to go.

43 – V

'GIVE ME THE FUCKING MONEY, give me the fucking money,' the bog-eyed mong was shouting at me. 'Where's my money? I want my fucking money!'

I wasn't going to give him any money. I was sure to hell I hadn't taken his money either; that didn't mean James hadn't, though. I wondered if he had hoovered up his coke or disappeared with his fancy women; perhaps he wanted reimbursing for them. Either way his strange accent and highly strung nature was vexing my spirit, which didn't take much effort considering the lack of sleep and quantity and quality of narcotics and alcohol I'd consumed.

'Give me the fucking money, you cunt.'

It was like he was shouting at me with a strange Chinese–cockney or Pakistani–Glaswegian highbred accent. The face didn't fit the voice. His thick, curly, black haired, white-faced, bog-eyed, middle-class, private-school-boy-wannabe-gangster, hard-man voice just didn't work, and I didn't like the cut of his jib. I was intrigued and yet disgusted. I should have walked away yet I was temporarily frozen to the spot. I was cornered yet in a wide open space.

And where the hell was James? Most probably watching somewhere with this bloke's money, bitches, coke and a big spliff on the go; terrific, he'd be pissing himself watching me dealing with this utter bell-endimous.

The bloke came towards me with some sort of exotic vodka bottle. He tried to smash it to threaten me – not an easy thing to do on grass, he soon learnt; still, I didn't want to be hit by it, so I raised my arms in defence.

'I don't know what you're talking about, mate. I've not got anything of yours,' I said, slowly backing away. I noticed the festival security making a hurried beeline in my direction through the crowds, flashing torch lights; they were the fake cops.

'What's going on here then?' The quickest of them asked. *Nice bomber jackets – they look the part*, I thought.

'He's some sort of nutter,' I said, nodding at the vodka bottle, innocence written all over my face. They performed a quick double take, trying to access the truth, and he was bundled into the back of their van, spitting profanities, out of pocket and out of his mind probably. I certainly was.

What the fuck had happened to James?

I meandered back into the crowd searching for one man in one hundred thousand.

44 – FIRST LIGHT – SUNDAY – 4AM

I SET OFF A LITTLE BEFORE FIRST LIGHT. By the time I'd filled the boat, reset the alarm and got myself ready I could see my breath on the air in front of me. It was still too early to appreciate the mist rising over the canal, although I knew the swans had already set about their early morning munch and the coots were already busy dragging branches and toot wherever it is they drag their shit – I supposed it was for home improvements but couldn't be sure; all I knew was they hated the ducks and if there was such a thing as racist birds then the coots were the worst of the lot.

I loosened the last holding rope and got ready to start the engine. As the little boat drifted with the current I felt a cool chill lick my face and so zipped my jacket up a little more to cover my neck. I turned the steering wheel full lock, turned the ignition, powered up the engine – it bit first time – swung round a full one hundred and eighty degrees and I was away.

I knew the journey would take the best part of a day; I had done the journey a few times before by bicycle when Chloe and I went for bike rides. I knew there was no difference in going as fast as possible and in taking it easy. The canal only had one speed; I suppose it a bit like me. Blink and you might miss something, wait around long enough and sooner or later you'd be rewarded or at least get what you wanted or where you wanted to be. A bit like a bird feeder: you hardly get to see which birds are eating the nuts but at the end of the day something must be because you always need to refill them.

I had all the gear: the taser, the tools and the refreshments. Speaking of which, it was possibly time for another snifter. I got out my supply and racked up two lines in the shelter of the cabin. After polishing off the lines my face was hit with the fresh air blowing over the boat. Tears ran down my cheeks; I wasn't feeling emotional but felt an almost childlike sigh wash over me as I patted at my face.

It was a fairly straightforward journey bar a few locks where I may have to communicate with other people, but I'd hoped and planned to have been up early and had enough of a start to have reached the twenty-mile stretch of the Grand Union that had no locks, and therefore eliminate most of the chances of meeting too many people before the masses were 'up and at 'em'. Then, hopefully, all I'd need to do is a few nods of acknowledgement from under the protection of my cap to other passing boats or occasional fisherman or overly energetic joggers or overweight power walkers or even speeding cyclists. Quite why the passersby would greet me always puzzled me; when I was younger people used to say hello when walking up and down the street, but not so in the cities. People seemed caught in a time warp on the canals; everyone said hello as if all were sharing an adventure and you might be the last friendly face before they disappeared into the wild. Not everyone was that friendly, though. I had noticed a few Eastern Europeans who were possibly searching for their next meal, maybe a swan or carp or even a pike; they were all on the menu today. They would skulk around in little groups, guzzling cheap extra-strong cans of larger any time of the day. It seemed we could turn a blind eye to the British water boat people tucking into the native wildlife, but Eastern Europeans were frowned upon.

As I navigated onwards I decided locks were a little like car washes. As a kid it all seemed so exciting and complicated and mechanical, and yet once you've done it a few times you just seem to go through the motions of hopping on and off the boat. You pull up, close gates, open gates, close gates and away.

A heron kept a beady eye on my progress before a careless water rat made the mistake of popping its head out of cover within striking distance. The heron had its breakfast menu sorted as well, impaling the rodent on its giant, sharp beak before flipping it up into the air and then swallowing it all in one; not much escapes the heron's appetite, and I wondered if the Eastern Europeans had considered eating them.

As I cruised on I watched an old Labrador squeeze out its morning turd as its owner talked loudly on his mobile phone. I couldn't see the point of using the phone: I could hear him for miles. When his voice was out of earshot and all I could hear was the chug of the engine I also saw two foxes jump into a hedgerow where they bickered in the undergrowth.

45 – FABRIC

I SUPPOSE IT COULD HAVE BEEN interpreted as an act of almost Judas-like proportions.

'Do you know him?' the bouncer asked James.

He looked me in the eyes and with nonchalant disdain replied, 'I know not this man.'

My hands were clamped behind my back: a typical security method of restraining people. I was marched to the manager's office. Behind me were two girls I'd hoped would be helping my evening, not pivotal towards probably ruining it. They were causing a commotion. People were staring.

We had been chatting in the club, James and I, hoping to get merry, as always on the lookout for whatever might come our way. Same old, same old: eyes searching dark corners of the rooms looking for shady deals, money changing hands, people popping pills. I guess we could have looked like undercover police as much as drunken druggies.

Then we were off.

'Pills, pills, pills?'

'I'll take six,' I said.

The two girls took the money and handed me the pills. Transaction completed, but within seconds the bouncers pounced and had me and the girls by the hands whilst James looked on vacantly. I was rumbled, and the girls tried to escape and ditch their stuff. I let the Judas thing go, self-preservation and all that. Seemed like a good idea, but right now I had six pills in my pocket and a bouncer holding both my hands and I was caught with the two girls who'd sold the stuff, but not James.

Whilst they were causing a scene and I was being escorted towards the rear of the club, I decided against trying to escape and being the bad boy being led away: no resistance, there was no swagger, no lip, no Charlie big potatoes, no gangster-wanna-be, just thinking, *How am I going to get out of this?*

I was frogmarched into the manager's office where the bouncers explained that I along with some girls had been caught dealing. At that moment another security bloke came in with a bag of pills in his hand, waving them like the FA Cup and pronouncing, 'Look what we found.'

The manager asked if they were my pills.

'They aren't mine,' I replied.

The manager, a mini Gestapo officer, said, 'The police are on their way. We do not tolerate this sort of business in our establishment.'

I thought, *You're kidding; you don't tolerate others dealing, you mean!*

'How do you know the girls?' Herr Flick asked. He looked the same age as me, but a weekly user of hard drugs and loud music; I recognised his stretched-out nerves and snappy, yappy attitude. He was probably quite quiet but then loud when he had a bottle of champagne at the bar, coke up his nose and fit girls at his beck and call, which I reckoned was most days if not weeks.

'I don't know the girls. I only met them tonight and was just chatting with them when you lot grabbed me. I don't know what any of this is about!' I said.

The girls were led into the room, looking flustered and pissed off, still resisting. The bouncer said he'd found the pills they'd tried to lose

The manager said, 'The police are on their way, won't be long now,' as if to reinforce his point to them and me. He looked around the room as if to add some importance to his words, seeking out the bouncers' knuckled-headed eyes as well for back-up before continuing.

'Do you know this guy?' he said, looking at me but speaking to the girls.

'No,' they said in unison like a couple of naughty school kids. They were actually pretty hot.

'We'll search you first then,' said the manager, indicating to bouncer number one to do the business on me.

Here we go, I thought. The bouncer patted me down and asked me to remove the stuff from my pockets. Bingo, my brain was working at double speed; a deception was my way out of this. I'd been patted down once; all I needed to do was remove everything from my pocket as naturally as possible and leave the pills in there. If they didn't pat me down again they'd think I'd already dropped them and hopefully I'd be in the clear. No evidence, no charge; as long as they didn't tell me to stand on my head. If I was lucky they'd just chuck me out. James would probably be outside milling around, waiting hopefully.

I pulled out my wallet, phone and chewing gum, then I rooted around in my other pockets for good measure.

'Wos in dat pocket dare?' the security gorilla asked.

'Oh, sorry,' I said, acting as innocent as possible, and pulled out a box of fags and a lighter to add to the growing pile of toot assembling on the table.

The manager checked inside my fag box. I found my tickets and some flyers and crusty old tissue in another pocket and flung them on the pile for good measure. I'd felt the pills with the tip of my finger whilst emptying my pocket. For a while time stood still and massive alarms went off in my head, but I ignored them, knowing they were looking at me for any indications. They missed that facial flinch. My only worry now was that some might be nestled in the tissue.

The manager briefly prodded at my worldly goods with a chewed biro and then asked the ape to check me again. *Fuck it! Here we go again.* This time when he patted me up and down I could feel the little fuckers pressing against my legs. I could swear they were burning a hole through my trousers and shouting, 'Oi, you daft fuckers, we're in here, near his balls, come and get us, fuck him, he's a dick, oi, oi, OIIIII!'

Whilst I was lost in my own mind the bouncer said, 'Nothing, boss, he's clear.'

'Okay,' said the manager. 'Are you sure you don't know these girls?'

'Absolutely positive,' I said, looking them in the eyes. I almost felt sorry for them; I felt like I'd done the Judas on them just like James had done to me ten minutes earlier. I reckoned the security had been watching them in the club. The police were on their way, they had been caught dealing drugs, hundreds of the fuckers looking at the bag they had. They had nothing on me, no evidence of any connection with the girls.

'Okay, he can go,' the manager said, looking at the bouncers but talking about me. Then he said, 'I don't want to see you again.'

The bouncer showed me out of the office. I expected to be led to the exit.

'Where do I go now?' I asked.

'Just fuck off!' The bouncer replied.

I walked back the way I had come, back towards the main dance floor. I looked over my shoulder to see one bouncer return to the room where the manager was with the girls while another stood at the top of the stairs watching me walk away. My adrenalin was pumping so hard my brain felt like it might explode and my knees were turning to jelly.

I'd picked up all my stuff. I hadn't lost a thing: I had six pills in my pocket and was walking back into the club, re-entering the fray. No harm done! I looked back again and the gorilla was still following me with his eyes. I guessed he wasn't entirely convinced I was as innocent as I maintained; perhaps they were going to be watching me for the rest of the night or for however long I was in the club – they had CCTV. Either way

I had best be careful. I made it back to where it had all started and James was still skulking about.

'What the fuck happened to you, mate?' he said whilst we had a little man hug.

I said to him, 'Not here, mate, let's walk and talk. And besides – I know not this man!'

We both laughed as we made our way through the throng of clubbers. I discreetly handed James three pills.

'What the... how the fuck?' was his reaction as he slipped them in his pocket.

'Don't say anything or do anything, just get rid of them,' I said whilst grabbing his beer and necking a pill. 'Listen, I think they might still be watching me and I suppose you as well. I suggest perhaps we double drop and see what happens. They might be a load of shit and this was all a big to-do over nothing. Let's go somewhere a bit quieter, one of the side rooms?'

On the way we grabbed a couple of bottles and two JD and cokes and I relayed the happenings over a few cigarettes and a few more JDs and of course another pill. We had a laugh over the Judas moment and the whole shenanigans and decided the pills weren't working and necked the last one. By my reckoning that was three in about half an hour. That's when they hit us.

The room we were in was playing a mixture of classic house and funk mixed in with old school northern soul. Before I knew it I was dancing like Michael Jackson and Elvis Presley's long lost love child and James was reversing in every direction possible. Shabam! We had arrived at the gates of Fooked City.

Hours started drifting by in a technicoloured sunset with florescent hail stones chucked in for good measure. Boy was I dancing now. Where was James? I remembered my partner in crime, me old mucker. He was sitting down, chewing an invisible pineapple. He was also rubbing his leg and someone else's!

I danced over to where he was sitting; it was easier dancing and moving than stopping and walking normally. I had forgotten what normal walking was; if I had to go anywhere now it would be dancing, wherever it was, right then it was necessary. So I danced over to him.

'You alright, mate?' I said, looking at him while still dancing, slightly bemused. I couldn't tell if he thought he was rubbing his own leg or one belonging to what he believed was a girl sitting the other side of him.

'Mate, you're rubbing this fella's leg!' I said, although noting the bloke didn't seem to mind; in fact he looked like he was rather enjoying it.

'James, you're rubbing his leg!'

'No, I'm not, I rubbing hers,' he said with through content, rolling eyes and a gurning, chewing mouth.

I wasn't entirely sure on the rules at this point. It was utterly necessary to dance, of that I was sure. I wasn't sure whether rubbing a complete strange man's leg believing it to be a woman's could be classed as a homosexual act or indeed a liberty. Perhaps the fact that James thought it was a girl's leg when in actuality it was a man's leg in some way excused him of the gay act, but the fact still remained that he was rubbing someone else's leg, presumably without prior consent. Although I figured they were both consenting adults. James generally wouldn't be the type to get touchy-feely with strange men, certainly not that I knew of anyway. Not that I'd have been overly bothered, that is, unless he was partial to rubbing my leg, in which case I'd probably have had to dance away or something. No, whatever way I looked at it, it might have been acceptable James behaviour had it been a girl he was busy leg rubbing, but it wasn't, it was this fella, and the fact he didn't mind kind of meant he was taking advantage of James in his leg-rubbing state.

I let out a massive, exasperated sigh before continuing.

'Look, you nutter, that's your leg there right?'

James looked gormlessly at his leg for a second and then back at me.

'And that's his other leg there, see,' I said, pointing. 'And you see that hand of yours there? It's on his leg, see!'

James looked at the guy sitting next to him, briefly looking into his soul.

'Oh, sorry, mate,' James said.

The stranger replied, 'That's okay, I was enjoying it!'

'See!' James said snappily to me as if he was now a master of leg rubbing and because the bloke didn't mind and quite enjoyed it actually that meant I was the one with the problem.

'Fucking hell,' I said, letting out another enormous sigh. I needed more JD.

46 – SULTAN'S GAFF – SUNDAY, 4PM

AFTER LOOKING AT THE PLACE on the internet and having been past there before with Chloe, my levels of anticipation seemed remarkably in check. Perhaps it had been the coke, but I was feeling self-assured and calm, almost matter-of-fact about the whole thing. Yes, I was going to do this.

I moored the boat up about a hundred yards short of the house. I'd have to remember to swing it round when I left; thankfully it wasn't a narrow boat as I'd have hated trying to do a U-turn in a hurry in one of those.

I put on my black Timberland jacket and black cap and walked towards the home of one of the richest men in England. I wasn't armed as such. I had the taser I'd got from Millwall Mike, but apart from that I was going into this with good luck and love on my side and was simply hoping to perhaps re-home some unappreciated relics. His house was littered with priceless treasures – I'd read about it – and they were famous and unloved. I reassured myself that not everything in the world was priceless, though, and although he wasn't usually in at the weekend his nonchalance and security protected him from normal, everyday worries. I doubted he would miss anything I happened to rescue; after all, he had more money than sense. He was worth billions, his house was worth millions, his dynasty would be worth billions, yet he couldn't see the worth of insuring or protecting his house. He would have been out clubbing the whole night before, probably spending the evening competing with any other millionaire who happened to be in the club that evening, like most weeks, both trying to outbid each other in wasting thousands of pounds on bottles of champagne.

There would only ever be one winner, though. That night the competition had been two premier league football club directors. Wads of cash were thrown into the excitable crowd of clubbers; security guards joined the revellers on their hands and knees scrambling around on the floor, looking for the unwanted readies. In a move of breathtaking arrogance the club manager was told to move a table of celebrity girl band singers to allow more room for desperate gold diggers and bleached-blonde, high-class whores to attempt to relieve them of some of their unwanted cash. Each time a ten-thousand-pound bottle of bubbly was purchased the DJ stopped the music to allow the bar staff to perform a firework display. That night, after the club had begun to bore him and his entourage had filled to the required numbers, he was going on to Vegas via his private jet where he was due to buy another thoroughbred race horse.

I scampered up the garden, hugging the conifer-lined edge. At every wall, of which there were three, I ducked down, checking I hadn't sprung any security traps of which I was unaware. I hid behind a well-manicured, miniature pine tree. The lawn was damp and recently cut; I guessed the gardeners must come every day. It was either a surprisingly barmy warm evening or I had a mild case of the alcohol sweats. I wouldn't normally be running around wearing a hat and coat and was sure I could easily have fallen asleep in that weather without them and woken up feeling confused in the middle of the night as fresh as a daisy. Was I feeling tired? I couldn't tell.

I couldn't see any dogs; the crazy paving gave way to my pitter patter as I streaked towards the light of the house. I stopped for a second to pick up a big stone and put it in my pocket. *Am I really going to do this?* I thought. I shook my head like a dog as I tried to remove the idea from my mind, casting the doubts aside. In and out, what could go wrong? More to the point, what did I have to lose? I decided the geezer was a prick and nothing more to me.

47 – THE END AT THE END

STACEY HAD WARNED ME: 'Be careful, these pills are seriously strong. I don't want you going mental and getting me or my other half in any trouble.'

Double dipped or something, twice as strong as usual, yellow callies or Mitsubishi turbos, either way they sounded perfect to me. I appreciated she was doing me a favour and didn't want to be stuck with the thought of me locked up in a nut house covered in drool for the rest of my days, busily chewing my shoulder or trying to get behind every radiator for as long as I lived.

'Only take a half,' she recommended, 'these are like double strength.'

She could have said wash it down with Cinzano and lemonade for all the good it did. If someone said do half, I'd do one; if someone said do one, I'd do two.

We were at The End courtesy of Peggy. We had been friends since school; she was one of Sarah's friends and we had stayed mates through the years although all my other female relationships had gone to pot or fizzled out. She had been involved in clubs for years. First at Turnmill's when the Chemical Brothers were resident DJs during the Heavenly Social period before the shift changed and welcomed the Trade punters. I'd usually got out of the club just before Trade got going, making the most of my evening at the Heavenly Social. There's gay clubs and nights and then there's banging hardcore gay clubs. It wasn't hardcore in the dirty sexual type of way with blokes fisting each other all over the show; it was hardcore in the sense that they were completely mental, totally off their tits and on a vibe that was so intense you wouldn't find it in normal clubs. I couldn't relax there for sure unless Peg was with me the whole time, although I loved the music. On the door you would be handed a Teenage

115

Mutant Ninja Turtle card or a top trump card, and your super hero strength defined your status as a VIP or guest list or regular clubber.

Hayden, Adam, Tom, Bob, Ryan and I ventured around the chill-out room and main dance floor, scoping out fit girls or likely suppliers of additional substances. We'd drunk a fair few beers in the local pub beforehand and were now switching to JD and cokes and vodka Red Bulls before entering the water stage of the evening.

I'd been down my sock and retrieved my special, super-strong jack and gills. I ignored Stacey's advice and popped a whole one whilst the others set about sorting themselves out.

As we wandered around the club, drinks in hand, I gradually became focused on nothing more than Hayden's back. It was as if I had become The Terminator or The Predator and I couldn't lose my target. As we walked away from the calming Balearic beats of the chill-out room and bar towards the banging main room I lost my target. I was also losing my grip on reality. As I searched for Hayden and the others the green lasers fired out from the projectors became solid blocks of substance, and all around me light became a motley kaleidoscope of patterns, green whirling shapes of paisley and black, building blocks that created real matter itself. I wasn't *at* The End, this *was* The End. Everywhere I looked nothing made any sense and yet it was crystal clear. I was part of The Matrix and an extra in *Tron*, I wasn't on earth as we know it any more, I was much higher. I'd left our realms of existence; I was now a visionary seeing uncharted landscapes. If a spaceman discovered new planets with life they wouldn't look like some burnt-out rock, they'd look like this: this was heaven of the future. If Lego could represent light beams then that was what I was seeing. Lego and psychedelic mottled snake ties made up of fluorescent and effervescent colours, magpie and jay feathers and dancing peacocks, luminous socks and shoe laces and big marker pens scribbling pictures in front of my eyes, industrial paint pots spilling light through my mind.

'God is that you? Are you doing this? Where the hell am I? How long have I been here? Where is here? Who am I talking to?'

As I gazed around the room, blinking to try to make some sense of it all, figures appeared in the darkness, people sitting in chairs in corners. I made out a light up ahead; perhaps light could help me figure out what was going on. It might be a bar: I needed a drink, and it might clear my head a little. My mind still felt detached from my body; as I walked it felt like I was continuously one step in front or behind myself. There was me and there was me. Somehow I'd left a part of myself behind and it was struggling to keep up. *Is it my soul?* I thought. I looked around. Perhaps my soul was my ghost and I'd lost my soul at The End. I searched around for myself but it was difficult because I was walking on a bouncy castle. Faces emerged from the darkness and then quickly vanished before I could ask if they had seen my ghost. The white lights were getting brighter, wider and bigger – were these the pearly gates? I wasn't sure if I'd been walking for days to get here, wherever here actually was. It looked like a space bar. Perhaps I'd travelled from space to drink here. It's simple, you see: you just go to The End and venture onwards. I needed a drink. These other beings seemed to understand, and I'd travelled through space, you see.

'JD and coke, please,' I called to the intergalactic alcoholic beverage supplier. I hoped they sold JD in space.

Leaning forward, I tried to rest on the bar; unfortunately my feet were still a few steps behind my body so I ended up in a sort of half-standing press-up position. My feet took the hint and joined the rest of my body, enabling me to stand up properly. I gazed around behind the bar, hoping to grab someone's attention, slightly concerned that I had done already and everyone was ignoring me. I puffed like a horse or an impatient old person in a post office as I waited for the drink to be delivered. Had I already ordered?

A man or angel turned up with my drink, so I quickly asked for another, but requested a double this time, and drank the first while I waited. After producing a few more horsey puffs he returned and asked for 'Benign pond plays'. I figured it must be a space amount and wasn't sure I had the right currency. I offered what I had in my pocket, which turned out to be a receipt which he wouldn't accept.

'Nine pound, please,' he said again, looking a little angry, so I rooted around for my wallet. I passed him a ten-pound note which he graciously accepted and then he was gone.

My feet had decided to take control of the situation and returned me to the press-up position on the bar. I obliged by doing a couple of bar push-ups; it seemed the right thing to do, almost polite, as a token of my gratitude for the sterling effort the staff on the intergalactic space bar had shown.

I picked up my drink, took a sip, let out an almighty horsey puff for good measure and went back into darkness towards the public melee. I was soon weaving my way through bouncy castle land, holding my drink like the controls to my body which were now either one step behind or in front. I decided the faces that were emerging from the darkness were potential drink-spilling foes; my sole mission was to protect the JD. I opted for a cyber-dimensional karate chop and horsey puffs as a subtle reminder to keep well clear. It seemed to be working: the faces I saw seemed to smile and be happy although I wasn't messing around – it must have been nervous laughter at the sight of my karate chops and horsey puffs. It didn't matter: the JD was surviving and I was making progress on my mission. What was my mission? The music was aiding my descent for sure as I wandered around the club, half dancing, half targeting likeminded fools likely to risk taking me on in a cyber-galactic karate standoff.

I stumbled across Hayden and the other lads.

'Alright, you fucking nutter?' Hayden said whilst immediately entering into a karate fight and chopping me on the arm.

'Fuck,' I said. 'You're not supposed to actually hit me!'

'There are no rules in space,' he said as I took a mouthful of my JD.

'Where have you lot been? I've been looking for you for ages. Fuck knows where I've been!' I said.

'You've been standing over there,' Hayden said, pointing at the wall. 'We've been standing next to you the whole time, until you went to the bar, that is.'

'What the fuck happened to me? I was off my tits,' I said.

'Yep, you were staring at the wall for over an hour.'

48 – WITH MY BACK – 4.30PM

WITH MY BACK TO THE COLD GLASS WINDOW I pressed up against the partly illuminated building. I could hear rumbles inside but was sure it was my hyped-up senses and paranoia. I certainly couldn't discount them being the dishwasher or the heating clicking on or something left to its own workings whilst the house was deserted. I decided I was making excuses and my paranoid mind was deliberately delaying me in an attempt to take over and stop me doing something stupid.

I took a deep breath, counted to three and went to whack the brick against the window. At the very last moment I remembered my gloves in my pocket and as the brick hit the window I had virtually stopped my hand moving, so the window cracked like a spider's web rather than imploding. I put my leather gloves on, which had been a pressie from my grandad, and smiled at them insanely. With the pane partially shattered it was easier to break the glass without making one massive crash. I felt like I'd been quite lucky. Once the window was clear of jagged shards I tucked my jeans into my socks and stepped through. I was now in enemy territory. My heart felt like it was beating too hard. In the past after exercising or consuming illegal substances it had beat extra heavily, but now I could hear it in my ears like a big drum from an orchestra reverberating through my brain and body.

I felt faint for a second, like I needed to lie down. What the fuck was I doing? I wanted to lie down just for a minute to catch my breath and re-evaluate what I was doing. I knew what I was doing: I was losing my bottle. I was in someone else's house uninvited. I was looking at someone else's belongings, deciding what I was going to take to become mine. I was breaking a commandment.

I edged forward, away from the window. The kitchen didn't look or smell how I had imagined it. I expected to see lots of gold-garnished taps and the heavy odour of spicy cooking lingering in the air with bongs and pipes and Persian carpets and woks and cauldrons bubbling. Instead I was in a clinical blue kitchen with stainless steel punctuated by chrome. It reminded me of a chemist lab where puppies are experimented on by companies selling expensive skin cream. It was modern and minimalist, designer and boring, and in my opinion not homely but cold and sterile.

I decided he was a puppy killer and edged towards the door that would lead through the hall and into the lounge. I couldn't be sure but I felt like I had been in the kitchen for about twenty minutes and what was meant to have been a quick smash and grab had already taken too long. What was wrong with me? Why wasn't I hurrying? I had to get a wriggle on.

I was moving as surreptitiously as I'd ever done.

The kitchen had a bar area used, I guessed, to serve meals. It had high metal stalls like you get at McDonalds. I noticed one seemed to have been left out of kilter, and also a pan drawer was half open.

49 – THE RETURN OF POND LIFE

WHEN I WAS TEN I WAS GIVEN a pair of budgies. Sunny and Snowy were their names, on account of one being bright green and yellow like the sun and the other white and blue and grey like the snow. Snowy was always my favourite; he was by far the friendly of the two. Sunny was the more skittish but by far the better flyer. It was at times impossible to get her back in the cage unless Snowy called her back. Snowy was quite fat. When we went on a family holiday Nan and Grandad looked after them for me. They put the cage out in the garden on a nice summer's day and a cat attacked the cage. Nan maintained Sunny got away but Snowy, being fat, stayed in the cage. I always had my suspicions that the cat got Sunny.

When Snowy finally died I was twenty-five. I had no idea as a ten-year-old how long budgies live. I went through puberty and several relationships, two schools, two colleges and several jobs. I spent more time with my budgie than most of my family, all my girlfriends and most of my mates! Snowy wasn't quite as obedient as a dog or as needy for cuddles and attention as a cat, but still his little whistles and chirps whenever I walked into the room were like a rock to me during the most testing period of my life. Truth be told, when he died I was devastated.

I never wanted to or would keep a bird in a cage again. I had, however, got some fish in a small tank that I hoped would keep Snowy company during the days before he went to the big feathery heaven in the sky. Years after Snowy had passed away and my fish and I had witnessed several upgrades in living quarters I finally managed to fulfil a promise and set my little finned friends free. Old One-eye, Jimmy the Eel, Sucker, Big Silver and Goldie and all the other little dudes.

After buying my first house with a decent sized garden I set about digging a hole. It wasn't a well-thought-out hole placed discreetly to one side of the garden or out of the way in a secluded spot shaded at the back under the old elderberry tree. Nope, it was slap bang in the middle. I wasn't content with a little hole either. This would be deep enough to bury an elephant. When it reached my knees I dug out, creating a platform, and then continued tunnelling down through London's finest discarded masonry, clay and mud. The second level was as deep as my waist and the last perfectly deep enough to bury a body or two. That was what the neighbours must have thought. A nutter had moved in next door and was burying something or somebody. When I was finally happy with my pit I carefully patted down the sides trying to flatten out any uneven, jagged edges and then I lined the pond with the black butylene lining. I installed a pump and filter, purchased water lilies and plants, filled the pond and set my fishes free. None of them would ever die floating at the top of a fish tank without seeing the sunrise and the moon appearing at the end of the day.

Their only worries now were lack of food (I wouldn't be chucking in any more half-eaten chicken wings for them to polish off), droughts and cats, and even those I wasn't entirely convinced were day-to-day worries a fish in a pond suffers from. It was truly a liberating experience watching the little dudes swim away freely and something I imagined biologists and naturalists savour about setting free a nearly extinct species reared from a foetus in a crazy breeding program in Timbuktu!

I could have spent hours sitting by the pond watching the fish getting on with their routine business. I guess that was why I liked fishing so much as well. It wasn't necessarily the catching the fish I loved, it was the sitting, almost at peace with the world. My favourite time was in the summer on a warm yet rainy day, under my umbrella.

I had been watching the pond and enjoying the sun on a barmy English summer's day whilst lying in a hammock next to the water's edge. It was quite a large hammock: Chloe's parents had given it to me and it was plenty big enough for us to be able to cuddle up and spend lazy summer afternoons relaxing there.

I had made myself as comfortable as possible by bringing down a few tinnies and a packet of balti mix, cigarettes and my telephone. I had no reason to move for the foreseeable future. I drank myself to sleep and the hot sun knocked me out and whisked me away.

I woke up with a start. What time was it? Where the hell was I? Had I missed the football? What was going on? All the usual questions my confused head tried to answer before letting me progress with my life.

I tried to lift my leg out of the hammock but it didn't want to let me go. The frame came alive and catapulted me straight into the pond before tipping over and covering me and the water's surface with its material. For a moment I was completely submerged with One-eye, Jimmy the Eel and all the others. I had entered their watery world. I watched as balti mix sank around me and the fish went into a feeding frenzy, oblivious to their new, massive visitor. If you put balti mix in a pond its every fish for himself. It's a fish eat fish world. Empty beer cans and a pack of cigarettes floated past and then my phone, which sparked me into life. I tried to stand up but everything was slimy and slippery. I tried to pull the fabric away from my head as I couldn't see the water's edge. I was being murdered by my pond and the hammock was in cahoots. It wasn't supposed to end this way.

With all my might and a massive roar I thrust myself free from the pond; thrashing and frantic, I managed to drag myself free as a worried looking neighbour clambered over my fence to lend a hand. When she was finally able to control herself again before breaking out into another fit of hysterics, she said it was the funniest thing she had ever seen.

I also decided then I'd never keep fish in tanks again, as well as birds in cages.

50 – MASON – 4.20PM

MASON HAD BEEN SITTING in the kitchen when he noticed me running up the garden. At first he panicked. He grabbed a saucepan from the kitchen cupboard and crept to the hallway as he watched the figure creeping around the side of the house. In fear, he snuck away from the kitchen. Not sure of his options, he considered hiding in the cupboard under the stairs. In the end he waited in the hallway, only remembering the gun in the lounge cupboard drawer at the last moment.

51 – CHLOE

CHLOE AND I BECAME GOOD FRIENDS AT WORK. My colleagues knew I harboured stronger feelings and aspirations than merely being working associates; they even went so far as to say I had no chance with her at all. I thought this was a little strong. She was in a long-term relationship and although she had never indicated she wasn't happy I remained undeterred. At work we were like a pair of budgerigars chirping away to each other. Sometimes I didn't even know what we were talking about until we were halfway through a discussion. We chatted shit endlessly and effortlessly, and as far as I could tell this was a necessary ingredient in having a decent, long-lasting relationship. My mum always said, 'Faint heart never won fair lady', and I figured I'd lost enough girlfriends to others in the past so it was about time I got involved in the act of stealing another bloke's loved one.

My optimism was given a further boost at a drunken office work party that went on all night and resulted in a group of us ending up crashed out in a hotel room near Old Street where our offices were based. Chloe was receiving some unwanted attention from a sleazy head hunter. I had decided the guy was a grade A dickhead earlier in the evening, and the opinion was reinforced when he was so consumed by catching his prey that he'd seen his Porsche get towed away rather than be prised away from his target. Even his pretty female sidekick seemed to be assisting his mission. I was convinced he was so determined to get with Chloe he didn't care about his car or anyone or anything else. I was sure if he couldn't win her over sober he'd get her drunk and then try. I did everything I could to ensure she didn't fall into his spider's web. If I couldn't have her, neither could he. He tried his luck one last time at the hotel but his advances were lost in translation. A phone message relaying his room number should she be interested would never be passed on, the operator decided.

Once the flames went out of the party, the coke ran out, the alcohol wore off and the curry went cold in its aluminium containers we all crashed out and Chloe and I curled up in bed together. Nothing happened; we just held each other doing spoons. That was enough: I couldn't sleep a wink. It was the second happiest moment of my life; having Chloe next to me asleep, together.

The next few days at work I was on fire, I was walking on clouds. I believed she really did like me, I had a chance. She had chosen to sleep with me rather than the sleaze or Asif or Dermott. She might just have felt safe with me I supposed, but who cared? It was all about me. My detractors were wrong; surely they could see now they were wrong as well? I didn't bother asking for an updated evaluation of my chances. I knew I was right. I was in love with her.

Then, just when I felt like my life was getting better and I was really beginning to get close to Chloe, she handed in her notice at work. I was utterly gutted.

It was my youngest sister's twenty-first birthday and there was to be a fancy dress party. I wasn't really in the mood, but Chloe insisted on dragging me to the costume hire shop at Old Street right next to our work. She seemed determined to be as nice to me as possible up until she left the company. I just wanted her to fuck off. I felt betrayed, let down and angry at her. I was acting like a spoilt kid who wasn't getting his own way. I couldn't help it. It didn't occur to me that perhaps she was leaving because perhaps I was getting a little too close to her and it wasn't fair on her long-term partner.

I went to the party dressed, inspired by Chloe, as a seventies-style pimp. I looked really cool, man. I guess I looked a little too good as I pulled one of my sister's friends and the next day she moved into my flat in Finsbury Park where she stayed for the next month. By the time we had split up Chloe had left my company. The memory of her hearing me describe my conquest the week after the party stuck with me. I thought I saw a little hurt in her eyes when I bragged about my sexual endeavours whilst being egged on by my other male colleagues. Perhaps I was being bitchy on purpose and had gone too far; it was her fault, though. Maybe I couldn't see it was a final act by my detractors to manipulate me and to further derail our relationship. They didn't want to see me prove them wrong and saw another opportunity to ruin our chemistry.

Things would never be the same again.

Before she left I helped her set up a hotmail account in the slight hope we would stay in touch. I also carried out her boxes of personal belongings to her car on her tearful last day. We didn't have a leaving party, as she usually organised those sorts of things, and although she looked sad to be changing companies I also thought she seemed a little jealous of me, almost resentful that I had moved into another relationship and was glad to be seeing the back of me. I was angry that I wouldn't ever know what she was thinking and that every girlfriend I ever had from that moment on I'd forever compare to her.

52 – BOOM – 4.33PM

As I PUSHED THROUGH THE KITCHEN DOOR, determined to get a move on, I saw a brief shadow flash like a blur before me. It was one of those slow motion moments, a delayed reaction, a sneeze that had pronounced itself on the scene moments earlier, the nanoseconds that accompany the falling glass that was knocked by your hand, the inevitable crash and shattering of splinters. In this case it was the saucepan. I saw the shadow and my natural instinct was to flee, duck, hide, protect, then the flinch, the defensive duck, but I was too slow. Instead all I felt was a ping ringing in my eardrums, falling, dust, light shadows dancing like ghostly images all around me possessing my body, forcing me down, burning my lungs

I blinked, my eyes working like a camera. My brain was unable to process all the information. Bleeding, pain, confusion reigned. My fingers sought splinters, shards of light piercing me, searching for a reaction, clawing, scratching nails, a feeling, ringing in my ears meeting a crescendo. Sight fading, dust everywhere, light and dark all at once. *What the fuck is happening?* My brain was banging. I wanted to run but couldn't move; I was in a hole. *Can I cough?* My eyes were burning, tears of grit. My teeth were jagged, sharp. My tongue felt massive. It had a mind of its own. *Go free, tongue, live your life, my time here is over.* Fucking ringing ears. Swallow, *I've got a pineapple in my thro*at. *Move fingers, blink, move wrists, two blinks, and a swallow, throat is on fire, move arms and shoulders. Nothing seems fine and not broken. I'm all smashed up. Move toes, feet, ankles. Nothing is fine. Move legs, they don't feel too bright either.* A stab of pain as a wolf chews on my leg. All sensory perception was now focused on my leg. My teeth no longer felt jagged, my eyes no longer burned. My ears stopped ringing. Now my heart was beating, anticipating my hand as it reached down to the wolf chewing at my limb. I couldn't move but the brain focused on the sticky, bloody-faced, viscous creature biting and clawing at my wet, stinging leg. The fumbling touches from my fingers sent electric shock waves to my brain. All other emotions and feelings and thought were eradicated momentarily as my consciousness tried to compute this new anomaly.

'Fuck, I'm fucking fucked.'

I couldn't help but think it was all over, and yet I understood this might well be the first signs of panic, so in reality only the beginning, only I wasn't panicking. I drew on my inner strength, my steely determination, my sheer stubborn-mindedness. *I must look at the wolf. I must move. I must try to get up. I must succeed. I must follow the plan. I must try to flee. But first I must kill the wolf.*

When I came around I felt sick and had a feeling of utter confusion. Had I been dreaming all along? I wasn't sure what I was waking to find; like in the past when I had woken up to find a massive scar on my face or a swollen wrist. I struggled to make sense of the ceiling and felt suddenly lost. I wasn't at home and in bed. I wasn't in familiar surroundings. Water was dripping on my forehead but I couldn't get up or move in any direction. My arms were stuck by my side and I couldn't move out of the way of the dripping. As I blinked my blurred eyes clear a face came into my vision. Smiling, triumphant and yet twisted with a nasty glare. It was a face I recognised although it was different, distorted and bloated with age. He spat again and it landed on my head.

'Mason! Let me up, get off of me, please!' I said.

'Don't be daft, you broke in here. It's my job to hand you over to the police or my boss. Either way, you ain't going nowhere!'

'Come on, you idiot, we went to school together, we were mates. Don't do this, let me go and I'll just fuck off and leave you to it. Let me explain – I only wanted a look around. Surely we can work something out, right?'

He poured a bottle over me but no matter how much I struggled I couldn't get out of the way of the water. I felt like I was drowning. My brain was banging and I was stuck.

Mason was laughing. He poured some more water from a jug into a plastic bottle.

'What you going to do now?' I asked, hoping to at least get out of this position.

'I'm going to play with you; at least until I hear what my boss wants to do with you. He might want me to keep you here so he can play with you as well.'

Any doubt in my mind that Mason might have changed didn't last long; he was a grade A cunt when we were kids and it was quite clear not much had changed in the years in between.

53 – RING MY BELL

I HAD A PHONE CALL A YEAR LATER out of the blue from Chloe. My heart stood still and I momentarily forgot how to speak.

She had left my life and I had tried to move on and now she was back.

'Hey, stranger, how are you? Do you want to meet up for a drink tonight? Are you free, that is? It would be good to catch up,' Chloe said.

I just stood by my desk looking around the office, searching for words, excuses and inspiration to help me speak.

'Errr, well, yeah, I should be around, erm, that would be great, I should be able to make it.' I was not cool and subtle but quite desperate and overly excited. I tried to persuade myself I hadn't really sounded all those things; it was no good, but I didn't really care. I was all those things. That's how she made me feel.

As it gradually sank in she wanted to meet up I decided it could have been West Ham vs Millwall in the FA Cup Final; it didn't matter – I would be there no matter what. We met at the Bricklayers' Arms pub on Rivington Street; she was with her friend Alison. They had regularly met up for girls' nights out on Wednesdays when Chloe had worked with me and tonight I was one of the girls. Tonight they had invited me. When the two of them got together they really did go for it. Alison lived right in the middle of Hoxton in an amazing warehouse conversion – she had been there since before it became cool – and every bar and club in East London was on her doorstep. We drank until we were battered. Alison was playfully flirting with me and she and Chloe took turns speaking in different West Indian, Irish and Scottish accents, gradually getting louder and courser. We laughed until our cheeks hurt.

I walked the girls home. Chloe was spending the night at Alison's and I accepted their invitation to come in for 'one for the road'. Alison decided I should stay as well and pulled out a futon in the lounge. After some deliberation I again accepted, although it seemed a little silly as I didn't really live that far away in Finsbury Park. As the girls got ready for bed I changed my mind again and decided to leave them to it and head home. I gave them both an innocent kiss and a cuddle goodbye and said I'd love to see them again sooner rather than later and headed out into the night.

As soon as I'd left the building and was walking up Kingsland Road I regretted my decision. Was it me or had Chloe been watching Alison flirt with me? It probably meant nothing, but I was sure I'd seen something in her eyes. It probably really did mean nothing, I tried to convince myself as I passed Herbal nightclub. There was no queue, just a bouncer in a long black jacket looking up and down the street, looking slightly chilly and bit cheesed off. I picked up my phone and called Chloe. She answered straightaway.

'Hi, Chloe, it's me. Listen, I was just thinking, do you fancy a dance?'

'Erm yes, what, now?' she said.

'Yes, now,' I replied.

'I'll be down in a second.'

I put the phone back in my pocket, turned around and started heading back towards Alison's place. In no time at all Chloe was walking up the street towards me.

'Where are we dancing then?' she asked, and that moment took my breath away. She wasn't supposed to be here. She wasn't supposed to have said yes. All these things that were happening right now were all dreamland things; they didn't happen in real life. I struggled to keep ahead of the situation.

'Erm, Herbal,' I said, remembering there was no queue.

I paid for us to go in and once we'd had our hands rubber-stamped and smeared with an inky tattoo we made our way down the dimly lit stairs of the club. The metal doors that reverberated in time under the power and pressure of the bass yielded and our bodies were washed by a solid wall of sound. Herbal always made me happy because it always felt a strangely lucky place as far as I was concerned. It was one of the few places where honkeys like me went and some nights were in the minority, but never once in the times I'd been there did I feel out of place. Well, apart from the time I had to rescue Slim Mike from the toilets because the local dealers thought he was serving up on their patch and pulled a gun on him; I guess that was partly the reason it felt lucky – I was lucky to have got out of that situation unscathed. I'd been there a fair few times looking like a stereotypical white City boy twat straight from work via a good few pubs, still wearing my suit, and still managed to have as good a time on the dance floor as any of the clubbers who'd travelled to London especially for a night out. Admittedly perhaps my attire was a little too formal.

The music was typical deep and dirty progressive house with a smidgen of drum and bass, just like I'd have requested had I been dining at a musical restaurant at that particular time. We ordered a couple of JD and cokes and skirted back around the main nucleus of people congregated on the dance floor. We quickly found our dancing feet and in no time at all were moving in unison with the crowd, every now and then sharing smiles with random people or those in search of the toilet or bar or those seeking lost or new dancing partners.

Out of nowhere the DJ dropped the volume and the crowd looked towards him like customers at McDonald's who've just learnt there are no more breakfasts available. The DJ introduced a young lad who I decided was quite possibly old enough to be my son. The crowd grew slightly restless as if in anticipation of the next boring child prodigy or squeaky voiced MC; he looked quite geeky and nobody expected much entertainment. I decided the kid didn't even look old enough to be out and about at that time of night, and whilst he was introduced to the crowd I scanned the club, looking for his guardian. Once the boy had everyone's attention he began his set. After a succession of rhythmic squelches he announced his name and everyone went nuts. He then started to beatbox and gradually the DJ joined in and one and all in the club went bonkers.

The lad had an orchestra and drum machine hidden somewhere in his gullet, and with the support of the DJ the rabble were whipped into a frenzy. Chloe and I were swept along as well, waving our hands in the air in time with the mob. I found myself moving in sequence with Chloe. Gradually we were getting closer together; I couldn't tell if she was reversing towards me or if I was edging closer to her. We were engrossed, watching the entertainment, dancing with the throng and whooping, when I realised my hand was on her hip. It stayed there for a while until she turned round and then we moved closer together until we kissed and at that specific moment I was transported instantaneously to the top of a hill somewhere a million miles away deep in the countryside on a starry night alone with Chloe looking over a sleepy village and then a thousand fireworks were let off and I realised we were kissing. This was the kiss, the one that meant more to me than anything in my life had ever done before. The happiest moment in my life. I held her tight and we kissed some more.

The music came back into our consciousness. I realised when I'd heard it before I was listening on my own, but now, as I heard it again moments later, we were hearing it together.

54 – TWISTED MINDS – 5.20PM

'Do you ever get it so bad, you see a girl walk past with such a sexy arse you just want to fuck her? You want to bang against a window and shout out to her, *Do you want to fuck?* Come on, admit it; I know I do. I have: that's how I met your Sarah.'

'Fuck off, Mason,' I said. 'You're just weird; you always were and always will be. Nothing but a creep. I'm not being funny, but what have you done since school? You told everyone you had a little one, but where is he now? You said your missus is dead. That's bollocks as well; everyone knows she ran off with someone else. Don't give me the same sob story you told everyone else. We all know what went on. You were happy to milk the attention, saying she'd snuffed it; you were pleased as punch people believed you and went along with your bollocks. Sob stories galore, you were made for it.'

'It's not true, fuck off,' Mason said.

But I continued. 'It was like winning the lottery, being able to say your missus had died. All those single mums desperate to lend an ear. All you had to do was lay low for a while and then move…'

'Shut up or I'll kill you,' Mason said.

'Let me go and I'll shut up,' I said.

He didn't, so I continued.

'You're a cunt, Mason; you always were and always will be. You should have killed yourself when she supposedly did. What did you do when you saw people you knew? Hide? She would only have died or made herself ill to escape you anyway. You blamed it on cancer. Fucking cancer! The only reason she would have got cancer or wouldn't have fought to survive it would have been to get away from you. She would have smoked herself to death. Imagine having to be seen in public with you! Look at you, all milk bottle skinned; you look disgusting. Have you never heard of a sun bed?

Join some of those freckles up, ginger twat. And what's even worse is that you didn't even realise she could do so much better than you. She was a nice girl and you ruined her. You never heard that saying "If you love someone, let them go"? Instead you were jealous, possessive and paranoid. You forced her away and ruined that relationship. What's wrong, you going to cry? Let me go and I'll shut up, Mason.'

He didn't, instead he stamped on my face, not hard, just as a threat of what to expect if I carried on. His face masked the internal anguish I was causing. He would react soon. I thought he might have started crying, but he looked mad.

'You could have appreciated her but you never did. Instead, you took her away, knocked her up, mentally drained her and took her for granted. You ruined her life. Now you're left with a kid who'll never know her mummy because you were such a nasty twat. You probably still think she was in the wrong for leaving you no matter how much abuse you dished out. You could have helped out and supported her instead of worrying about your next benefit cheque. You let them both down, just like you let your family down. Do you ever even go home and see how your poor mum is doing with your kid? You treat your family like your friends: you let everyone down like you let your mates down when we were kids. No wonder you disappeared. Why are you back anyway?'

Now it was Mason's turn; I could see he had snapped.

'It's been known, in some places, once the usual holes have been used for rape, you can cut someone and make new ones. You ask me how I know these things?'

I didn't say a word; I just looked at him staring down at me and thought, *Freak*.

He went on. 'I can see it in your eyes. At the same time as wanting the answer you know you might regret asking, so you lie there and stare at me, trying to bluff your way out of this situation. See, you don't know me, you know fuck all about me and where I've been and what I've done. You're trying to bluff me right now with your mental steeliness; it won't work, though. You see, your eyelids flicker at the thought. The repulsive nature of the subject offends you and you're ill at ease. You could scream and shout but I can cut your tongue out. You ain't going anywhere. Your options are limited. You'd do incredibly well to get out of this in one piece. In the end it might be better to be dead.

'Would you like to live the rest of your life minus your tongue? Your famous tongue that could talk its way out of any situation. Bollocks. You'd be mentally scarred, physically spent. That's what I'm going to do to you. Physically spend you. You won't be able to tell anyone anything. They won't want to know the gory details. If I cut off your fingers and hands as well, you'd be a gurgling mess. Imagine how long it would take for you to tell your story with blinks of the eye or nods of the head. You ain't going to be doing any sign language. I could hold my scalpel blade right in front of your eye, yeah, I could take off your eyelids first then you won't be able to blink or do nothing but watch whatever I do to you.

'I could bum you; you'd probably like that though...'

'Fuck you!' I screamed and thrashed but got nowhere.

'Oh, am I getting to you now?' Mason said.

He was right he was getting to me; he'd got me with the scalpel and the eyelids shit and now the talk of bumming was the icing on the cake. I'd had enough.

'We should have let you fall off the train,' I replied.

55 – ICELAND

Iᴄᴇʟᴀɴᴅ ɢᴇɴᴇʀᴀʟʟʏ ʜᴀs ᴀɴ ᴇғғᴇᴄᴛ ᴏɴ ʏᴏᴜ or me or anyone. You drink in pubs, clubs, bars and restaurants. You drink some more, you go out for a cigarette, maybe lots of cigarettes. You get drunk. You go to another club and get even drunker. You go out for another cigarette and it isn't dark. You drink so much that you can barely stand and the thought of another smoke makes you feel sick but you go outside and it's still not dark. You aren't sure if it's tea time or breakfast; the only certainty is that it isn't night-time. It was never night-time. Only it is, according to your watch. It just never got dark.

I wasn't sure if sometimes it was always dark. I was barely coping with the whole lack of darkness; I would have been beside myself without any light either. We seemed to be continuously partying surrounded by arguably the most beautiful girls in the world. It was a chilly oasis where the days never ended. We were there for my cousin Henry's stag party; during the day we'd been hiking all over icy glaciers and now we were out clubbing all night in Reykjavik.

As always seemed to be the way with me, our numbers had dwindled until I was left with only the most determined of pissheads. After the last of our crowd had sensibly headed home we tried a few more bars and searched for one last hot spot; me and my new wing man Mark, whom I had only met for the first time a little over twenty-four hours earlier. Not that that mattered in our continued pursuit of beautiful woman, music and – paramount in my mind – recreational drugs. I could have been paired up with Jack the Ripper and we'd still have been mates for the evening.

Somehow we ended up in a gay club, not that Mark seemed to have noticed, not until I pointed out that the place was well short of the beautiful girls Iceland was fast becoming famous for.

We cut our losses and jumped into a cab. Our laughing, mental taxi driver was a cunt. In most countries the purpose or role of a taxi driver is to drive you from one point to your requested destination, A to B. In this particular cabby's case his job description meant he would charge you and then go straight to point C. This bastard drove us around for a while whilst laughing and chatting gobbledegook in Icelandic before abandoning us nowhere near where we wanted to be. He royally stitched us up, laughing all the while.

Mark called after me, 'Where are you going?'

I was pissed off and pissed up and had decided we were staying just over the brow of the hill at the end of the rural street where we'd disembarked and along which I now found myself swiftly ambling along.

'Wait here with me and I'll try to get another cab to take us back via town. I think I remember the way,' Mark said

He was probably right as well, and I shoulda, woulda, coulda listened but I had already passed the point of no return. I was in the place I went where no matter how stupid the idea, there really was no reasoning. I was walking and I didn't give a fuck if he was with me or not. I knew where I was going, the taxi driver probably hadn't stitched us up and I wanted to trust him for no reason at all. My legs worked fine anyway. How hard could it be? I was staying just over the hill at the end of the street along which I was cruising so I speeded up, determined to prove my point and get home first.

I got to the end of the street, which was like any other from American movies like *The Goonies* or *Teen Wolf* where the paper boy throws the pre-rolled newspapers onto the driveway, aiming for the porch or dog. As I walked the over the brow of the hill the initial familiarity of the street gave way to a steady stream of similar looking roads and neighbourhoods that all looked the same and foreign. Mark would be long gone by now. My initial confident stride developed into a drunken jog and in turn my boozed-up musing became determined rants, *one more hill... one more street*. I knew we were staying in a hostel somewhere near the coast, and I was sure if I could get there or at least see the sea I'd have a slight chance of finding my way home.

On I jogged, rapidly becoming sober, tired and very annoyed. My feet were aching from hiking all day and dancing all night and now running. The houses and suburbs gave way to an industrial area with factories and giant parking lots. Still, it was light at least, and still on I jogged. I didn't seem to be getting any closer to the coast and I hadn't seen any taxis for hours.

I decided to try to use my phone. I didn't have my cousin's number and didn't know anybody else's in Iceland. I tried calling 118 118, disregarding what country I was in; it might work and at least they might be able to give me a taxi company number in Iceland if only I knew where I was. No joy… I sent a few random text messages in frustration.

My sister thankfully suffered from insomnia and didn't mind giving up on a little lie-in to help rescue her stupid lost brother wandering around somewhere in another country. She sent my number to my cousin Henry's sister, who then contacted her sober stag of a brother, informing him over breakfast I was still at large meandering the streets of Iceland in the middle of nowhere. By the time Henry had contacted me my phone's battery had been on its last bar for quite some time and was now regularly beeping at me, letting me know it was no longer capable of assisting my rescue mission.

Thankfully he found me on the outskirts of town with nothing but wilderness between me and the glaciers and then probably the Arctic. I was totally knackered; I'd wandered and jogged over ten miles away from where we were staying. I got home after a slightly emotional reunion to be told the group was leaving for the day's activities in half an hour. I'd already missed breakfast and it was understood if I didn't fancy going along. I figured half an hour's sleep would be plenty. I was still feeling drunk anyway. A little sleep and I'd feel right as rain again.

As soon as my head touched the pillow I felt myself drift away, succumbing to fatigue. I closed my eyes for a second, smiling at the thought of Henry's heartfelt rescue of me. I guessed it might be a highlight of his stag party and certainly something to tell the grandchildren once we were old and haggard. We had grown up together and had known each other all our lives, and we'd been through certain trials and tribulations only people who've know each other all their lives experience. I rolled over, trying to get comfortable, and rubbed my heavy eyes.

'Right then, time to go!' Henry cheerfully announced.

I had only blinked and it was time to go? I figured I might get a chance to grab forty winks on the coach en route to wherever we were going.

'Where are we going?' I asked, hoping for some respite.

'White water rafting,' Henry replied.

'Terrific!'

We were going white water rafting! As far as I could tell it might be the best hangover cure ever invented; if nothing else, it was sure to wake me up after less than half an hour's sleep.

I drifted in and out of consciousness on the bus, occasionally aware of my name and tales of my exploits being related. Questions were raised as to the extent of my sanity; nothing should be taken for granted, I supposed. I heard Henry and one of his friends saying that if the opportunity arose that they'd prefer to do the white waters in a canoe rather than as a group on a raft; a few others agreed; the majority thought they were mad. So I volunteered to try the canoes as well.

'Jesus, we thought you were asleep!' Henry said.

'No, just resting my eyes. I'll do the canoe as well, please, should be fun. And wake me up when we're there. Cheers. Night night.'

The group laughed, at me or with me, I wasn't sure. I didn't care. How hard could it be?

Half asleep I clambered off the bus, following everyone into a large wooden and concrete log cabin in the middle of a dull, cold, drizzly, green, barren landscape situated besides a slow, muddy, brown river. The room was full of damp-smelling wetsuits and puddles and industrial-sized hairdryers. Feeling weak, I changed into a soggy wetsuit. I tried to eat a chocolate bar I'd stashed in my pocket but felt sick straightaway. I ate an indigestion tablet instead and burped up a chalky gas bubble.

We had a brief safety talk. I tried to pay attention. I must remember to cross my arms over my chest and keep my toes pointing up should I fall out of the canoe, yada, yada, yada. I was switching off instead, concentrating on trying to get some heat into my freezing feet. It was all basic stuff apparently that everyone with any canoeing experience should know; unfortunately I had no experience. I was beyond novice. I'd been in a pedalo in Menorca. The beautiful Björk then spoke to me about how to get someone back in the boat should they happen to fall out. She recommended holding them close to the boat and then pushing them right under the water so the buoyancy in their life jacket forced them upwards – this would then give the would-be rescuer the necessary momentum to grab the person and pull him or her back to safety.

I broke myself from her Nordic spell and, with her words of wisdom ringing in my mind, I put on my helmet and fastened all the zips of my now cold and soggy wetsuit. I wasn't feeling any better, I was feeling positively awful.

We were told to form two groups: those who wanted to do the rafting and those mental enough to do the canoeing. The rafts, of which there were four, took teams of twelve, and since leaving the coach our party had been joined by several other similar sized groups of likeminded people who were all excitedly getting themselves ready for the experience as well. The rafts were led by the instructors who said that those in the canoes were to follow them so they could watch out for us in case we paddled into any difficulties.

I was told to team up with another person as the canoes were two-people vessels and that way they could put someone with limited experience with someone who had substantial knowledge. I ended up with Mark again. He had managed to grab a couple more hours' sleep than me. Although I had been a dick and left him in the middle of nowhere, he was still being alright with me, so I decided I thoroughly liked the cut of his jib. He was fully aware of my lack of experience, but was more than happy to risk life and limb in my company, so I was more than happy to have him as a shipmate, though I was unsure as to whether he had any boating experience either.

Mark suggested I sit at the front and just keep paddling and he'd sit at the back and try to steer. It all sounded like a perfectly reasonable plan, but as we edged out into the icy water following the instructor's raft my feet turned to stone and every pebble and rock on the river bed seemed to find the arch of my foot. I was relieved to get out of the frozen river and onboard our vessel. The water was so cold I felt my brain rattle inside my head as my blood turned to ice. I jumped into the boat, feeling less human and more like someone living in a bad dream. The canoes were about ten to fifteen feet long and made out of an extremely tough inflatable material. Once you jumped in you sort of knelt in them like the native Indians.

Within twenty seconds of setting off and just about coming to terms with how to go in a straight line, I had cramp in both my knees and my hands felt like I was going to inevitably get blisters and my body felt like it wanted to be sick. I was tempted to piss myself in an attempt to warm up. I would have done it but I was afraid my penis, which was now so cold it would have resembled a button mushroom, had retreated to a safer haven along with my bollocks, which would now be situated somewhere around my neck! I was so cold. Mark behind me encouraged me on, as if sensing I was on the verge of slipping into hyperthermia. I don't suppose he was feeling much better.

'Just keep paddling, seriously, no matter what… you keep paddling,' he shouted.

Like I have anything else to do, I mused to myself, unable to think of any witty reply.

'Just leave the steering to me, you keep paddling,' he continued.

We kept a steady distance from the raft in front. The space between our canoe and the raft we were following didn't seem to change whether I paddled hard or allowed us to be pulled along by the current. Still I carried on the illusion of following Mark's instructions and rowed away. I noticed my cousin and his fellow canoeist expertly ploughing alongside their companion vessel. *The flash bastards*, I thought. I momentarily lost my balance and bearings whilst I was busy watching them. I saw them respond to the instructor on the raft and drop back a little and then the raft they were following came alive with a chorus of excited whoops. I looked a little further along the river and noticed the white water disturbing the previously calm ebb of the river. The current seemed to pick up and my paddling seemed now to be forcing us on even quicker.

I stopped paddling for a second, taking stock of the situation. Surely this wasn't right? We shouldn't be here. Why was I here? What on earth was I doing? Should we turn around, make for the shore; carry the boats past this bit. That would be safer, right? I watched as the first raft and then the canoe were swallowed up by the rapids before being spat out once the river had tasted them and decided it didn't like the taste of their morsels. The passengers bounced like a rodeo rider on a bull on water.

'Don't stop paddling. Really go for it. We need you to paddle to get us out the other end. I'll watch the rocks and steer. Don't stop till we clear the white stuff, right...' Mark urged.

Fuck this, I thought. *Far better to brace myself and hold on for dear life. We're gonna fucking sink, oh shit, oh shit, oh shit.*

'Paddle,' Mark urged, and my arms came to life like a jump-started engine. The beautiful Björk at the back of the raft we were following briefly caught my eye and I imagined she fleetingly gave me a little smile.

'Charge,' I shouted as we went in face first. The nose of the canoe went down into the depths of the river before reappearing again even quicker. I dug my feet into the side of the canoe to stop myself being buckarooed straight out of the boat. I spat out a mouthful of water and, listening to Mark's encouragement, kept paddling. I couldn't and wouldn't stop now until we were well clear of this madness. We were being buffeted and chewed up and thrown around, enveloped in the frothing, freezing spray. I no longer cared. I was paddling.

Mark was screaming; he was laughing. Was he mad? I realised we were doing alright and began to relax and try to feel the current and understand the flow of the river; I wanted to learn to respect it. Was I bollocks? I concluded and concentrated on paddling as hard as I could until I was well clear of this utter lunacy. *What sort of mad people enjoy this sort of thing? Seriously, you can die doing this shit...* I cursed as we battled through a few more dips and swirls and came out the other side into calmer waters. Everyone was cheering and splashing the water with their paddles in their various vessels, and as we caught up with the raft we were following we realised we had survived and got caught up in the jubilation. We had survived. That was quite fun, I supposed. I guessed I felt slightly exhilarated and slightly less hungover, which was a massively welcome change.

I tried to stretch my knees and, turning around, said to Mark, 'That wasn't so bad, eh? I could do with a coffee now. How you doing?'

Mark just nodded towards the raft we were following as Björk beckoned for us to keep up, so we gradually started paddling again. I hoped we were going to be heading for the banks of the river; this was quite fun, but I'd had enough now. That's when I noticed the current again seemingly gathering pace and the background din created by the next set of white waters angrily protesting at the rocks that were like teeth piercing their raging watery skin, jutting out of the river like immoveable objects, pointing towards us, sucking us in, getting ready to scoff us down and tear us apart.

'Start paddling!' Mark shouted over the furore. This looked a lot busier; choppy even. I could see the raft we were following had kind of got wedged in a swell; it was slowly turning in on itself like an inflatable sandwich.

'What do we do?' I shouted to Mark. We couldn't wait for them and I was worried we would smash into the back of them. Mark couldn't hear me anyway. My job was to keep paddling; his was to steer. If we smashed into them it would be Mark's fault. *This is why it's dangerous.* I was getting angry. This was a silly idea. People could get hurt.

As we were buffeted around Mark's voice seemed to be punctuated by the water swilling around my helmet, shooting in and around my ear holes. I couldn't understand a word he was saying. Up and down we went. Occasionally I'd use a paddle to try to push us away from a rock, but it was no good: either our weight or the power of the river or the speed we were going at weren't going to be altered by a plastic paddle. I did all I could do and that was to continue rowing and digging my knees into the side of the vessel for all my worth.

We hit the next fall straight on like a pole vaulter. I thought at any minute I'd see Mark sailing over the top of me as we seemed to grind to a sudden halt in the river. I waited for a moment and half, expecting Mark to shout, 'Keep paddling!' I started up again, paddling as hard as I could. He didn't say a word.

We pulled clear of the whirlpool I was worried we were going to disappear into, so I turned round to check on him. He had gone. I kept paddling for a second more and then looked back again, hoping my mind was playing tricks. Nope, he had definitely gone.

I pulled my paddle into the boat and looked around the river. 'Fuck!' I shouted, thinking I didn't want to be involved with a death like this. Not with a hangover. Not now.

Then he popped up a little way from the boat, desperately clawing his way in my direction. I used my paddle to try to pull him closer but we were entering another set of rapids and all I was doing was hindering him, so I dropped the paddle back in the canoe and grabbed hold of his life jacket. He clung on to the canoe's bindings and we were again tossed down another set of waterfalls. I held his arm over the side of the boat and hoped to God he didn't get trapped between the rocks, the boat and me. As we came through the first set of rapids I was relieved to see his body and head still attached to his arm.

We entered a brief calm section, which led to another white water section. I was feeling it was only a matter of time before I lost Mark, and noticed the instructors noticing our man overboard. But they couldn't do anything to help us. They were entering the next set of falls.

I shuffled back to the middle of the boat and grabbed Mark's shoulders, pulling him parallel with the canoe. I shouted, 'On the count of three.' As I counted out the numbers I pushed him up and down a little, getting ready for the third final big push. 'One, two, three.' On three I pushed down with all my weight, hoping he'd hit the river bed and be able to bounce back like a salmon in a stream. I nearly toppled in after him but somehow righted myself as he popped back up like a cork, and using his momentum I half hauled him back into our canoe. I reached down, grabbing between his legs, hoping to grab a limb. The wetsuit made him feel like I was wrestling with a slippery seal and I was dangerously close to using his bum crack as the only point to get a decent grip. He was totally shattered and lay limp, half sprawled across the side of the boat. I used all my remaining strength to tug on his life jacket until he slumped into the bottom of the canoe. He lay still for a second, I guessed in shock.

'Are you alright, mate?' I said, feeling a nervous, excited smirk grow across my face. I wanted to laugh. I always wanted to laugh at moments like this.

I looked around for the paddle; it must fallen out when I was trying to pull Mark back in. We were slowly rotating towards the next of rapids and were already floating sideways down the river. I then saw one of the paddles in the water not far from the boat, a little over arm's reach away. I splashed and clawed at the water, desperately trying to get it back.

'What on earth are you doing?' Mark asked, shivering from the bowels of the boat.

'Trying to get a flipping paddle back,' I replied desperately.

Mark looked up and over the edge of the boat, immediately understanding our predicament. It looked increasingly likely that he was going to be back in the water very soon. To make matters worse, we were now going down the river backwards and we had run out of time to retrieve the paddle.

I stuck my feet and knees as deep into the side of the canoe as possible, grabbed the bindings, looked at Mark and said, 'Here we go again.' I then realised I'd forgotten about my hangover.

56 – JEALOUS HATER – 5.45PM

'I'LL FUCKING KILL YOU,' Mason said.

'No, you won't. You're a fucking pussy,' I said. 'You're acting all hard but you're a bottle job!'

He didn't like that. 'No, I ain't,' he replied. 'I ain't scared of you, or any of the others. You're nothing. You and the others thought you were all that and so hard and cool, but you weren't nothing. You were just the same as all the others I've met over the years. You didn't give a fuck about anyone else either. All you cared about was going out and meeting girls and getting off your tits.'

I could see tears welling up in his eyes.

'You weren't part of our group, Mason. You don't know what you're talking about. You would have brought us down if we'd allowed you to hang out with us, and you were an embarrassment,' I said.

Tear rolled down his cheeks. 'You think you know me?' he screamed. Real emotion in his voice. 'You don't know me! I was the geezer you all left behind. You all moved on with your new girlfriends and cosy little in-group. Happy because you were all sorted. You were all allowed to stay out late, had the cool clothes, and when you went anywhere all you talked about were the things you and your girlfriends and you all did at parties and things without me. I wasn't even allowed to stay out late. I sometimes snuck out late to see if I could find you. All you ever did was go on about the fucking girls. Fucking girls. It was all I ever heard. They were all so sexy. And I just had to take it. Me, Mason! The ugly ginger kid no girls fancied. My life was hell, but you lot didn't give a shit. You even took the mickey out of me dancing on my own at the school discos 'cause no one would dance with me. I occasionally chatted with a few of them. I don't know what you had said because as soon as I said my name they all ran off.

'Years passed and I wondered what was wrong with me. My brother had girlfriends and all you lot had girlfriends. That's what I didn't understand. You must have been the reason. You and James: you two must have turned them all against me. But why? Why did you fuck my life up? Eh? So that's why I moved away. I left the country and started again in Jersey. Even then I occasionally bumped into people who'd say, "Do you know James or his mate? You know, what's his name..." Of course I knew they meant you; everyone knew you two. No one knew me. They were always talking about you. You, you cunt. No matter where I went in the world you were hanging over me like a horrible ghost that had to ruin my life. I hate you. I fucking hate you.'

With that Mason huffed and stared at me with nothing but anger and hatred in his eyes.

'You have issues,' I said.

He hit the top of the chair and sort of roared at me in frustration. Spit formed in the corners of his mouth.

57 – A PILOT LIGHT GOES OUT IN PARIS

I'D BEEN OUT ALL AFTERNOON with some of my designer clients in the Soho. We'd drunk and eaten in the Masonic pub near the grand lodge in Covent Garden before hitting a titty bar in Holborn. My clients had decided they were as drunk as they could get on my expenses and called it a night, leaving me to return to work to grab my bag before deciding what to do next. I gave Georgee Paris a call to see if he was still around and whether he fancied a few drinks and perhaps a smidgen of mischief. We were supposed to be meeting up on Saturday for the football but nevertheless arranged to hook up. He had already organised the mischief by the time I'd got back to meet him. I left him in the pub next door as I nipped back into work to sort myself out.

I ran up to my desk to get my bag and check my computer for any emails. There was nothing of interest on my computer; well, at least nothing that couldn't wait till Monday. I thought I'd take advantage of the peace and quiet to rack up a couple of lines at my desk while I had the chance. It would be far easier here than in the toilets of some bar or club later and I hadn't seen anyone on the stairs up to my floor so no one knew I was at my desk. The floor was empty and the coast was clear. I set up two lines using my Oyster card, rolled a twenty and hoovered up the first. Then the toilet door opened and the phantom shitter, the bastard everyone hated, appeared. What the fuck was he doing on my floor at this time of the evening using my toilet?

If I didn't move he might not notice me. I cupped a hand over the gear on the desk. I was desperate to sniff my nose. I could feel crumbs of Charlie falling out every time I breathed. He noticed me.

'What you doing here, Pilot Light?' he said, coming over.

I swept my right hand across the table, hopefully removing any evidence, and in one movement tried to stand up, pinching my nostrils together like I had the sniffles before saying, 'Nothing, I just come back to grab my bag. Been out all afternoon with TGS Agency.' I bent down and grabbed my bag.

'Are you pissed?' he said.

'Probably,' I replied.

'Don't forget your twenty pound note or your Oyster card,' he snapped back.

Checkmate, hung drawn and quartered, busted, hung out to dry, good night Vienna, hello you must be the fat lady, will you sing me a tune? My eyes focused on the rolled note sitting next to the Oyster card with lumps of half-crushed powder embedded against the dark blue plastic.

'Yeah, right, okay.' I grabbed at them, putting both back in my pocket, and walked hurriedly past him.

'Have a good night,' he said, almost mocking me.

What the fuck would he do? What the fuck did he know? I guessed it was up to him now. He held all the cards. I was fucked if he wanted me to be. He knew exactly what I was up to. He could get on the phone right away and grass me up. I fumed all the way downstairs and next door into the pub where Georgee was waiting at the bar.

'You took your time, what's with the long face? You look like you've seen a ghost,' Georgee said.

'I've just done myself up like a kipper, haven't I!' I replied, before explaining what had happened.

'There's only one thing for it,' Georgee said, inviting my reply.

'What?' I asked on cue.

'We kill him and chop him up!' he said earnestly with a maniac's grin.

'Very funny,' I conceded before agreeing there was no point crying over spilt milk. What was done was done and I shouldn't lose any sleep over it. I had class As to thank for that. There was nothing I could do. I'd just have to deny everything if accused; it would be his word against mine.

We ordered a few more drinks and a couple of Jaeger bombs and then left the pub to play some pool in The Pool Rooms. The Friday night crowd mixed with drugs, cheesy chart music, pool and beer goggles gobbled us up and spat us out at around two in the morning. We got a cab to Old Street and danced till about six o'clock in the 333 Club before again being regurgitated back into the world. We must have scored some pills as hours were drifting by. We wandered the East London streets around Brick Lane as high as kites, drinking out of a box of cheap red wine. I don't know where it had come from; I certainly didn't remember buying it. Some twenty-four-hour off-licence somewhere had either sold it to us or lost it to us.

A Tibetan monk led us astray for a short time. He turned out to be a hairdresser but was kind enough to offer us a beer in his salon whilst his Oriental customers with Mohawks and undercuts silently scrutinised us from underneath asymmetric fringes. We left them to their lives and unusual hairstyles and continued with ours.

We had become nice, slightly strange, venerable drunks. I felt like an albino afraid of the light. Darkness had given way to daylight in a blink of an eye. When had that happened? I had no idea. Georgee looked better suited to darkness as well. We were vampires cruising the street in broad daylight, looking for some darkness. My face felt sunburnt as well, possibly from all the booze. I was conscious of what was going on but rapidly losing the plot. One second I was play fighting with Georgee, horsing around like Muhammad Ali and Joe Frazier, the next I was chatting with a skinny black crackhead fella, the next walking off with a slightly uglier looking hooker until Georgee rescued me.

When his back was turned I jumped on a 205 bus, thinking I'd be heading in the right direction towards West Ham from the city. Georgee would no doubt run after the bus and get on and meet me at the next stop or something; he'd find me somewhere somehow, I was sure.

I blinked my eyes and was no longer in East London...

I was wandering along a busy crowded road; my best guess was somewhere in the West End, maybe Paddington. How on earth had I got there? It was a bright sunny day, beautiful even. I was walking straight into the sunlight. I couldn't really see a thing. I didn't even know how I came to be on the street. I walked along, staring at the shops, looking for landmarks, desperate to get my bearings. My head was pounding, and I was dehydrated and feeling very confused. I battled against the shoppers as I muddled along, spinning down the road, until I found an Underground station. I fumbled in my pockets for money. I couldn't find my wallet. I checked the time. It was a quarter to three. That couldn't be right. I was supposed to be at West Ham. I should be in the pub with all the lads. I should have been there hours ago. I was never late. Everyone would be asking where I was. Why hadn't anyone phoned me? I checked my pockets for my phone. It was gone. I emptied my pockets. I had a fistful of change, my iPod, and no wallet, no phone and my fucking Prada sunglasses had gone as well.

I punched the wall out of frustration and shouted, 'Fuck!' A foreign family of Spanish tourists protectively pulled their young boy and girl closer to them. I tried to apologise, but it was too late. I'd scared them and damaged England's reputation some more. I purchased a Zones One and Two travelcard and ran, hustling myself as quickly as possible to the platform. I ran like a scruffy scarecrow. I jumped on the train and ascertained I was on the wrong end of the Hammersmith and City line but it would take me to Upton Park eventually. I grabbed a seat, put on my iPod, closed my eyes and shut out the rest of the commuters from my mind. Like an ostrich, I was avoiding any disapproving stares as I was utterly paranoid. Kings of Leon whisked me away into a semi-dreamland.

What on earth had happened to me and where had I been? Had I been kidnapped? Had I been mugged? Where was all my stuff? Perhaps Georgee had it. I hadn't gone off with a hooker, had I? I was sure I hadn't. I was tempted to put my hand down my trousers and feel my cock just to check that hadn't been stolen or left behind somewhere or still sticky with seedy aftermath. I opened my eyes briefly to check my watch. The game would have started by now. Would Georgee be at the game or still out somewhere looking for me?

By the time I got to Upton Park it was coming up to half-time. I ran from the station to the Boleyn Ground faster than any away fan had ever managed during the hooliganic period. I went to the ticket office and explained I'd lost my wallet and season ticket and somehow was miraculously issued a replacement. Unfortunately it was in the wrong part of the ground and I had to make my way from the Dr Martens lower / Bobby Moore end right the way round to the Trevor Brooking lower stand near the away supporters' end.

My mouth was so dry I could hardly speak. My face felt like it was burnt and throbbing. I was feeling like I was about to suffer a nervous breakdown and I had about twenty thousand people between where I wanted to be and where I was at that moment. I heard the cheer go up for the start of the second half and made my way along the concourse as far as I could go, getting as near to my seat as possible. I shuffled past the Carling-sponsored larger sellers – that proved slightly tempting; if only I had enough money. I went past the chicken balti pies that were simply food of the gods on any other match day – I felt my stomach angrily protest, when was the last time I'd eaten? Friday lunchtime! That was over twenty-four hours ago! On I walked past the ropey hot dog sellers that guaranteed dodgy gut within a few hours; even on my last legs these didn't appeal! I made my way into the stadium and looked out onto the pitch. I had a brief look at the score board: nil nil. I jumped over the divide that separated the two stands and quickly made my way behind all those standing in the row, saying excuse me and trying to be as polite as possible the whole time.

I finally made it to my seat, hoping for a hero' return. Unfortunately I could tell by Georgee's glare that I was wrong. I thought he was going to kill me.

'Where the fuck have you been?' he scowled.

The other blokes, Ryan, Thomas, Nick and the two Rich's I went with, turned around and gave me a half-hearted, almost sympathetic smile.

'Fucking chill out, I'm here now,' I said.

Georgee went to hit me but was stopped by Ryan, who was the fastest to react.

'Calm down, what on earth is your problem?' I said.

'Tell me to calm down once more and I'll knock you out, you prick,' Georgee said, fuming.

'Calm down, love, you can see he's off his pickle,' the fat bird that sat behind me every week chimed in. I looked at her, half smiling and half frowning. She was normally horrible to everyone. I wouldn't ever risk getting into a fight with her either.

'You can pipe down as well, love,' Georgee said.

'Charming,' she said.

'Why didn't you phone any of us?' he continued.

'I thought you had my phone!' I replied.

'Why would I have your phone?' he said.

'Because I thought, well, I hoped, I'd given it to you with my wallet and shades because I seem to have lost them all,' I said.

'You're a prick!' he said

'Why did you jump on a bus and piss off all of a sudden?'

'I have no idea,' I said, feeling guilty and stupid instantaneously. 'Listen, I'm really sorry, but if I don't drink something soon I'm going to die. I feel like shit.'

'You're going to die when Chloe catches up with you. She isn't feeling well and hoped you'd be home last night. She's left messages with everyone. I didn't want to speak to her today and say I still had no idea where you were. Christ, you were walking off with a prostitute not long before you disappeared on the bus this morning. Seriously, what the fuck is wrong with you? Did you get mugged?'

I had no answers. The second half had already started and it was only when an effort went inches wide that I was able to ignore Georgee's interrogation for five seconds. The fat bird behind me patted me on the shoulder and passed me a bottle of half drunk diet coke. I was going to say I hate diet coke but instead I mouthed *thank you* and tried to blink the most sincere thank you I'd ever attempted before. I don't know whether it looked like that or a lazy attempt at fluttering my eyelids because she looked at me like I'd farted. Ryan lent me his phone so I tried to call Chloe. There was no answer. I'd try again after the game. I was sure she was fine; she was probably just pissed off that I hadn't phoned last night before staying out. She'd forgive me sooner or later.

I watched the rest of the game through rolling eyes and wobbly knees. Occasionally my mind was dragged back to the game but for the majority of the time it was lost trying to fathom what had happened once I'd got on the bus. What had happened to my phone and wallet and glasses? Had I put them down or was I robbed? Over and over again I tried to think back, putting together the pieces; trying to ignore Georgee who was begrudgingly right to be angry at me.

The match ended and whilst the others decided what pub to go to the fat bird behind me slipped me twenty quid and said, 'Give us it back next game, eh, you piss head.' I thanked her because I really didn't have any more money. She said, 'Piss off,' and called me a 'silly sod'.

As the crowd left the stadium I followed Georgee, Thomas and Ryan at a slight distance, mostly because I couldn't keep up. At any moment I could fall asleep: I was on my last legs; my head was in the clouds.

Georgee and Thomas stopped at an off-licence and grabbed a few tinnies. Handing me one, Georgee gave me a half smile and put half an arm round me. 'What we going to do now?' he said.

'I don't know,' I replied.

'We had a good night though, eh? Do you remember dancing with those girls in the club?'

I had no idea what he was talking about. 'I'll stay for a beer but I really need to head home and make sure Chloe is okay,' I said.

'I make you right on that one. She's going to be pissed off with you alright, and she tried phoning everyone to find out where you were.'

I said I would try to call Chloe again once we got to the pub, which I did. She wasn't answering for some reason, and I was struggling to finish my second pint. I kept falling asleep mid-conversation, and to make matters worse it was really hot and my head was pounding and I just wanted to curl up and go to sleep.

Georgee said he'd get me to the train and that I had to make sure I stayed awake. I asked him to send Chloe a message letting her know I was on my way home and said I'd catch up with him during the week. I got a ticket and a can of coke and put my iPod on again. I was determined not to get too comfortable before getting on the Metropolitan line. Once on that I could relax just a little as I was going pretty much to the end of the line. I made my connections and choose a seat in the corner at the front of the carriage, and as soon as my face hit the cold glass window I was away with the fairies.

I woke up again to find myself walking down an unfamiliar road in a strange neighbourhood all over again. Now I was really confused. Where the hell was I now? I must have fallen asleep and sleep-walked off at the wrong stop or something. I looked at a road sign – Latimer Road. It meant absolutely nothing to me. The houses, the roads, the signs – I could have been in Bulgaria for all the sense it made. I started walking again. There was bound to be a cab rank or a pub or someone somewhere who could help. Perhaps if I was lucky Chloe would be out looking for me and she would drive down the road any minute. I had to get home as soon as possible. I just wanted to say sorry to her and have a cuddle and then perhaps curl up on the settee together watching rubbish on TV.

58 – SABOTAGE

As MASON GLARED DOWN AT ME, spitting profanities in my restricted direction, I wrestled to free my hands and arms. My neck was stuck under the first bar of the chair legs; my body was directly between the four feet and my legs were sticking out the other end. The more I struggled the more he laughed at me, knowing I was pinned under the chair and his weight. I couldn't escape his menace. I couldn't move as he poured more water on my face, choking me under intermittent deluges. In slow motion I watched the water spill down towards me out of the light blue Perspex jug. As I thrashed and spluttered and spat water back towards him I noticed his arms and legs and hands were wet and his trousers too. I had a glimmer of an idea. Next time he poured water on my face I'd take as bigger mouthful as possible without swallowing.

As he poured I opened my mouth and filled my gullet until I nearly gagged. When he stopped and began his next verbal onslaught I spat the water back up at him like a fountain. Up it arced. I didn't have the power to reach his face but it landed on his lap and splattered the arms of the chair and his hands. I stopped listening to him arguing and concentrated on doing it again and again. If I could get him as wet as possible he'd either move of his own accord or I would move him. He did it a couple more times before getting fed up with me spitting back at him, so he stamped on my face, hard this time.

I tasted blood in my mouth from my busted lip. He'd missed my nose. Thank God.

I wriggled my hands into my pockets and found what I was looking for. I turned the taser on and waited.

I spat a mouthful of blooded sputum at him whilst wriggling, trying to get his wet hands to grab the metal. I imagined I'd only have one chance at this and had to make sure none of my body was in contact with the chair. He put down the jug and gripped the arms of the chair, staring down at me. He was going to stamp on my face again. Wet hands on metal. The plastic shoes on the chair should insulate it; only one way to find out. I fiddled with the taser in my pocket. He couldn't see my hands directly under the chair. I couldn't reach his leg but I could reach the wet chair legs. He wouldn't have a clue.

He lifted his foot to stamp on my face again and I touched the taser against the chair. As I fired I could hear the electric charge pump and crackle up through the metal. The snapping, cracking sounds seem to make Mason temporarily freeze and grip harder on the chair. As if confused by the sound, I watched as he grabbed harder on the chair and I saw his knuckles turn white like he was on a rollercoaster. I wasn't sure if it was working or not. I couldn't tell if it was the surprise or the strange sound that had made Mason grip tighter and lean forward in his chair, but the moment I stopped firing the taser he moved forward, as if to get away from the chair. I used his momentum and all my strength to push the chair with him. In the flash of an eye he was tumbling over me with the chair following suit, straight towards the kitchen cupboards, and I was scrambling up and grabbing the saucepan and hitting him and kicking him and punching him in an unleashed torrent of utter hatred.

He was out cold, lying in a wet, bloodied, bruised mess on the kitchen floor. I took off his shoes, pulled out the laces and tied up his hands and feet. I dragged him to the cupboard under the stairs in the hallway and shoved him in. I bent down and retrieved my cap, which lay where it had fallen.

I really wanted to get a wriggle on now. This wasn't going anywhere near as smoothly as I had hoped, although I had planned for the unexpected.

Mason might very well grass me up when he woke up so I might not make it very far in the future. Perhaps I should kill him then and there. Perhaps I shouldn't leave him in the cupboard. Maybe he'd use the opportunity to leg it himself, take a prize and start again somewhere different – either way it wasn't my problem. Or was it?

I wanted to get my picture and run. My lips felt swollen, I had a small egg on my forehead and my leg hurt from where the wolf was biting me or the chair leg was pinching. I felt pretty sick. But I had to do this, so I made myself go through the hall and into the lounge. I opened the door, slightly paranoid I was going to be on the receiving end of another flying saucepan. I'd been hit once with a pan and been stamped on; I already felt like I had the worse hangover I could remember. I doubted it would feel much better in the morning.

I then worried about whether Mason had phoned anyone. I didn't remember seeing a phone on him anywhere. He had been smashed up and soaked and zapped so hopefully he wasn't likely to use his mobile phone in a hurry, but whether he had used it whilst I was out cold was still uncertain.

59 – SHATTERED DREAMS

WHEN I FINALLY GOT BACK TO THE HOUSE it was getting late again. Chloe wasn't in. I called out for her but she didn't answer. I had given up hope that she was going to come and find me wandering the streets hours ago. Now it was my turn to start to worry.

I found a note on the work surface. She said she was feeling really poorly and had gone to hospital. Her note said please come to find her as soon as I got home because she was scared. She said she hoped I had a good night and that she wasn't mad at me.

Her note didn't say she was battling to stay alive and our baby was already gone.

60 – THE CALL – 6.13PM

As Mason came around in the darkness of the cupboard he struggled to release his hands. They had stupidly and hastily been tied in front of him and to his feet, so it didn't take too much effort to free himself. He had no idea what had happened but felt battered and bruised and also livid, even angrier than he had ever been about anything in his whole life. Then he heard noises outside the cupboard and, blinking in the darkness, worked out where he was.

There was no handle on the door and if he busted out he was sure to be heard so he had to sit tight and wait. He checked his pockets, looking for his phone. If nothing else he might actually be able to use its light to undo his feet. The phone was wet. He wiped it dry and switched it on. The screen was cracked and barely lit; it was impossible to read. He fumbled with a few buttons, trying to get a call to work, but nothing was happening. He was getting frustrated and desperate when suddenly it started ring someone's number.

James's sister had two strange calls that evening. She posted on Facebook about a weirdo who had whispered down the phone to her, interrupting her favourite reality TV show. Her mates gave her several suggestions as to what to do if he tried again. Several 'liked' the idea of blowing a whistle down the phone.

The number he had found was old friend James'. He had long since left the family home but his sister still lived there. Only when she answered the phone she didn't hear an old friend of her brother looking for help; she heard a weirdo. She hung up and he somehow managed to call again, but she hung up again and he wasn't able to get through any more. Mason was dismissed as a weirdo once again.

61 – DECISIONS DECISIONS

I STOOD IN THE LOUNGE. Two pictures stood out amongst many on the walls in front of me. Behind a big, old, wooden desk littered with family photos and cars and horses was what looked very much like the Picasso portrait I had recently read about being purchased for thirty-two million pounds. I'd loved my anniversary trip to Barcelona with my wife and seeing the picture brought back a flood of happy memories. It was indeed the last really happy memory I had of before everything had gone wrong. My mind drifted whilst I stared aimlessly at the portrait. It was like watching a TV programme about our life. It took me away to another time. I felt joy and sadness together until a cold shiver broke the spell.

I looked around the room. There were plenty of other pictures I recognised. A Giacometti and a bronze statue stood proud in the corner as if about to go off on a long walk on a windy day. This room was more like I had expected, a little like Aladdin's cave full of treasure. I half expected Sinbad to come in with some more loot. The wooden table was swamped in gold and Oriental style wonders whilst everything looked expensive and yet cluttered. I felt like an extra in the old *Laurence of Arabia* movie or something, and could have been in a tent in the middle of the dessert with a harem busy smoking hookah and lounging on thick Persian rugs eating Turkish delight. That's when my attention was pulled back to the stolen Van Gogh. It had been taken from an exhibition in Egypt. It must have found its way onto the black market where it had then been purchased by the grateful sultan via some shady agent.

It could have been fake, but what were the odds? It had only recently been stolen and the picture it had replaced had only recently been left on the floor awaiting its next allotted place.

I chuckled to myself. Should I take both? How could I leave a stolen picture? It wasn't even his in the first place. Perhaps I should replace the picture on the floor with the stolen picture? About eighty million pounds' worth of paintings was a little more than I had hoped for. Fuck it; what did I have to lose?

One painting evoked warm memories of my wife. I grabbed this one and the stolen Van Gogh off the wall. They fitted nicely under my arms, although the frames were a little bulky; but I had always liked big, old-fashioned frames almost as much as the pictures themselves.

I made my way back through the house, through the hall and past the cupboard. *Mason might wake up soon*, I thought. Still, the door was closed and he hadn't broken out and hit me in the face with a saucepan, so I hustled on. I stepped over the pan on the kitchen floor and felt my head wince subconsciously; I kicked the chair out of the way, noticing the mark on the cupboard door where Mason's head had made a greasy imprint. I gently put the first picture through the hole in the window and then stacked the second against it before climbing through myself. I then started running like a bird with two wooden wings.

62 – MASON'S FUMING – 6.28PM

MASON MANAGED TO KICK OPEN the downstairs cupboard door. He looked around the hall and went straight to the lounge. If he was angry before, when he noticed the two missing pictures he was positively seething. He had failed his job. He ran to the big wooden desk and fumbled for the key in his chest pocket. Ramming the key in the lock and pulling on the drawer, he nearly dragged the whole compartment clean out. He grabbed the blackish cloth shoe-bag and emptied it on the table. The Glock handgun fell out. It was already loaded with bullets. He switched off the safety and was ready to kill.

He raced through the house, gun held out in front of him, leading his way. Through the kitchen window he noticed his target running like the wind down the garden. He was hunting but his pride was battered. He had nothing but venom pumping in his veins, coursing through his mind. He had to stop this fucking liberty. He had to kill. He wanted to kill. Then he would be happy again. Nothing else mattered.

63 – KEEP ON RUNNING

I'VE GOT TO FUCKING STOP HIM, Mason thought.

Nothing can stop me now, I thought.

Mason ran through the garden, setting his sights on me. But he couldn't stop me, I was running free. Full strides, giant leaps on air, like the wind; I could run for miles like this. I was eating the path up in front of me. I was breathing in pace. My heart was pumping and the adrenaline was flowing. My hands and wooden wings helped scoop the air around me. I was the opposite of a bad dream: I was poetry in motion.

Along the garden I bounded. *Not long now*, I reassured myself. *I'll soon be away from London and its crowded, dirty streets*. I could almost taste home. There'd be no need to hide, no more eyes, no tears, everything would be sorted, and everything would be okay.

This is for you, my love. These gifts are for you.

64 – YOU SHOULD'VE SEEN THE OTHER GUY

BANG... BANG, BANG.

As I heard the third bang I was stung by a million bees. I went down like a toppled windmill; the pictures flew away from me like beautiful bin lids. Face first, I went down, sprawled in the grass, tasting its green in my mouth. I stayed still for a moment. Absolutely terrified. *Oh God,* I thought, *has Mason really just shot me?*

Frozen, I was concentrating on not moving. I wasn't sure if I'd been hit. In my head I checked my toes, feet, ankles up my legs past my knees, back and belly, my neck and head, fingers, wrists and finally settled on my left arm. It hurt like hell. I stopped self-analysing and steadied my breathing. My heart was pounding. I could hear it louder than ever, thumping in my brain. Each beat was echoed by a throb in my arm that burnt me to the core. I concentrated on the sounds of the water lapping on the edge of the canal. I could hear it kissing the boat. I had been so near. I was still so near.

I could hear feet running getting closer. It would be Mason coming to finish me off. Should I try to run again? No, I decided. I would freeze. I had to think quickly and one step at a time. If I got up to run that's what he'd be expecting. I didn't want to make anything any easier than it had to be. I didn't want to die having been shot in the back running away. I remembered the joke about the randy rooster waiting for the buzzards and decided to fuck the fucker. My good hand snaked under my body tentatively, feeling its way to my pocket under my groin. I felt inside: wrong pocket, empty. Fuck. I tried to move my other arm but someone had stuck a red hot poker in it. I sucked on my lip so hard I felt it burst and my mouth was filled with the taste of the iron in my blood.

The footsteps were getting closer now. Mason was slowing down. I guessed he wasn't sure if he had hit me or killed me properly after all. I could hear him shouting; he sounded pissed off and scared and very upset all at once. I wasn't sure as I could also hear a loud ringing in my ears. I let the blood dribble out of my mouth but concentrated on not moving a muscle. I tried to stop breathing. If he wanted to be sure I was alive or dead he was going to have to shoot me point blank or check my pulse. I hoped more than anything he wouldn't have the bottle to do either. Although a part of me didn't care. I decided shooting me in the back from a distance without any warning was more his style. It would take someone with bigger bollocks than him to shoot someone up close. Cold and ruthless. God, I hoped I was right.

He was right on top of me, circling me, looking at his handiwork, checking where the pictures had fallen. If he shot me again I was definitely finished. I lay dead still. Still trying to hold my breath. I hoped he didn't look at the arm wound too closely and decide to add a body or head shot. Although it hurt like hell I was sure it alone wasn't going to be the end of me. He kicked my leg. It hurt but I didn't move. No reaction at all. I could feel the gun pointing at me and was determined to ignore the usual reaction to pain. I couldn't move: it was life or death. All I could hear now was his voice, mocking and triumphant.

'See, this is what you get,' he was saying.

He rolled me over and I let my good arm fall free by my side. I stared, fixed, unblinking. The blood dribbled from my mouth added to the dead effect I had created. I still didn't move. I was seeing but not looking. My eyes turned to glass. I didn't move but felt the rage boil up inside me now, coursing through my veins, forcing more blood from my wounds. If I could have I'd have drowned him in my blood. A drum roll beat inside my head, starting to slowly gather pace. I held my breath as the shouting Mason leant closer still. His breath leapt like a ghost's from his mouth, dancing briefly before me before disappearing into the atmosphere.

Unbeknownst to him, turning me over had freed my pocket and my good hand had been inching its way into my pocket millimetre by millimetre until now it had reached its final destination and was embracing the taser like a long-lost lover. I flicked the switch, turning it on, and waited for the climax. Whilst Mason perched next to me, gloating and staring at me with his gun tracing around my body, I waited for him to drop it by his side.

I didn't have to wait long. The moment his hand dropped I went for him like a cobra. The beats in my head lost all rhythm and instead of percussion all I could hear was a noise like a steam train. The taser flashed up in my good arm, propelled with all the strength and speed I could muster. I smashed it into his cheek, keeping my finger on the pulse button, firing a steady charge into him. It was his turn now to go down again. The rolling break beat returned to my head. I used my good arm to get to my feet, rolling over and pushing myself up. I zapped him again for good measure. He let out a gurgle and a moan as the volts temporally paralysed him like an epileptic. I then set about kicking him in the face and stamping on him, over and over again, breaking ribs, until I felt like a kid walking on snow. I then concentrated on shattering his shoulders and hips. When they were smashed, I threw his gun into the canal. I put my belt around his ankles.

As I was about to pull Mason to the boat I remembered my arm. I had almost forgotten about it in the excitement. I raised my good right hand to my left arm and it felt disgusting, sticky, burnt and raw. I couldn't do anything about it now, so I picked up my belt and Mason's ankles and slowly but surely started dragging him one-handed to the boat. When I got there I jumped on the little vessel and pulled out some plastic sheets and the portfolio. I took them off the boat and laid them on the bank and him on the plastic. I ran back up the garden and grabbed the pictures; bringing them back to the boat one by one, I cut out the canvases and popped them in the large portfolio. But I couldn't leave those beautiful frames, so I put them back on the boat in place of the portfolio. As I passed Mason I momentarily caught a glimpse of his face. He looked just like the twelve-year-old I'd gone to school with.

I got back on the boat and pulled out a family-sized disposable barbeque and lit it. I returned to the boat again and grabbed the branch cutters. I then took off my jacket, wincing as the dried blood and burnt skin was separated from the fabric of my coat for the first time. I was tempted to jump back off the boat and give Mason another kick in the face because of the pain; it didn't seem right, though, to kick a man whilst he was down. Instead I just gave him a dirty look as he lay dead on the grass.

I checked the far bank. I wondered if the gun shots had been heard by anyone. I guessed it could have been a back-firing car or fireworks. I couldn't see anyone on the other side of the canal and they wouldn't be able to see Mason's body from there. The garden was obscured from view by the walls, rows of miniature conifers and landscaped features. I wrapped an old blue scarf around my arm and tied it as tight as I could manage with my mouth and one working hand. I felt sick and almost faint, like when I was younger and had pierced my ear. My wounded arm was feeling numb, and all the way down to my hand and beyond my fingers burnt with a pain I had never felt before. I looked at my blood-stained hand and tried to clench my fist; instead I was absorbed looking at the blood – some was still wet and I didn't even know if it was mine.

The barbeque was burning away fine even if it was quite a cold, damp evening not really ideal barbie weather. I took the branch cutter over to where Mason lay, spread-eagle on the plastic, and looking down at him. I placed the cutter over his right hand near the wrist and cut it off, and then on his arm near where the shoulder used to be and cut off his arm. I took him his hand and placed it on the barbeque, fingers up. Sausages on the barbie. I then did this to his upper arm, placing it in the flames to seal the meat. I heard his blood, fat and skin pop and spit in the flame. Hog roast. I did the same with his other arm, hand and both his legs and feet. Finally, once his limbs were all done I pulled his torso to the barbeque and sealed his arm and leg sockets.

I took his arms and legs, hands and feet and put them in the satchel compartments on my fold-up bike that was still on the boat. Lastly I took off his head and cooked his neck, leaving him smouldering away on the disposable barbeque.

I cleaned myself up as best as I could using wet wipes and rinsed the branch cutters and plastic sheets in the canal. I stuck the plastic sheets back in a bag on the boat and placed the torso in a heavy-duty black bin-bag. Finally I kicked his head off the barbeque and wrapped him in another heavy-duty plastic bag and chucked him on board the boat. I poured the used coals into the canal, hearing the satisfying hiss and pop as the heat hit the cold. I smelt the mist rising. Molecules of Mason embedded in my nose. I put the disposable tray with the other rubbish on the boat. I'd be able to drop that off in a bin later, I hoped.

Once everything was on the boat I considered going back to the house. It was empty, the pictures were missing, Mason was missing, there would be water on the floor in the kitchen, drawers open, would anything else tell a story? I had no idea. Perhaps it would look like Mason had staged a burglary, I really couldn't think.

I powered up the boat and pulled away from the sultan's house. Part of me just wanted to head home then. So what that I had someone's body chopped up on the boat; perhaps I could feed him to the fishes on the way home? It was a stupid idea. I had to do it right. I didn't have a clue what to do. I pulled the boat over and moored up again on the other side of the canal. How long did I have before someone turned up at the sultan's? Would anyone think to look right under their noses? I was panicking, not sure what to do with the torso and head. I took the bike off the boat. I wondered whether Mason would like to go to London Zoo to feed the wolves.

I heard a rustling in the bushes and froze. I couldn't believe it: I was busted. I looked towards the noise in the undergrowth and my adrenalin started pumping again. Flee or fight? A badger shuffled out, presumably attracted by the fragrance of the cooked meat wafting on the air. He edged a little closer and started talking.

'You going to feed him to the wolves?'

'That's the plan,' I responded.

'You'll never get his head and torso through the bars,' the badger said. I decided he sounded like Bob Hoskins. He then waddled back into the hedgerow as I muttered my thanks.

He still hadn't given me a plan for sorting out the head and body. I decided to leave them behind. In double-packed plastic bags I put them in a big rucksack and using plastic binding straps attached them to the anchor. I then dropped them overboard. My hand and arm felt utterly useless. Everything was taking twice as long as usual and everything hurt. To top it all off my head was feeling fuzzy and I was suddenly afraid. I wasn't sure what was scaring me, but felt sure eyes were on me, and I couldn't be sure they belonged to the talking badger.

65 – BICYCLE

I LEFT MASON'S HEAD and torso overboard firmly attached to the anchor. I stored away the branch cutters, picked up the heavy portfolio and put it on the bank next to the fold-up bike with laden satchels on the front and back wheels. In my pocket I checked the bunch of keys. Two for cars, two for houses, one for the boat and one for the storage space place.

Pulling the portfolio over my shoulder sent shockwaves down my arm. I needed more drugs and wouldn't be able to do this without something. I was feeling weak, tired and paranoid but couldn't see any other option. I managed to pull a little wrap of coke from my pocket and clumsily tear it open. I dabbed one finger in the white powder and rubbed it round my mouth. I dabbed again and tentatively touched my finger tip to the wound on my arm hoping the drug might have some medical benefit. It felt crispy and raw and came back red and repulsive.

My first attempt at riding left me face first in a bush lying in a crumpled heap, having crashed almost immediately. I had no strength in my arm and as the bike wobbled I'd got nervous and crashed into the hedge.

I tentatively picked myself up and reorganised through the pain. My mistake was not appreciating the uselessness of my arm; I had to try to stop making stupid decisions and make allowances for my disability. I had to calm down. I couldn't use my brakes as that put pressure on both my arms; I'd have to use my feet as much as possible.

I turned on the flashing lights and tried for a second time. It wasn't that it was dark, but somehow with the path now illuminated a little so I at least had somewhere, a destination, albeit barely three feet in front of me, that I needed to head towards. 'Follow the light,' I repeated over and over again. The more momentum I gained, the steadier the bike became.

Unfortunately this was counter-balanced by the ache in my arm and neck, trying to compensate for my useless side.

I trundled along. All was quiet, and I hoped I looked like an art student rather than a murderous art thief, but no one was around on the canal to ask. On I wobbled under bridges on my way into town. I could hear the Sunday evening traffic. London was still alive; it was never totally dead.

I came off the canal near Blomfield Road mooring. I stared up at the closed little cafe looking down on me, giving the strange impression of being in a foreign country. Perhaps I was. I'd been here before but it all felt different and alien. Tree-lined streets, big residential buildings. Everywhere looked clean; London was supposed to be dirty. Maybe I was in a parallel dimension. A car horn jolted my attention back and I struggled to control the bike as cars raced past. All of a sudden the world had pace and I felt like I was in a slow motion bubble. I stopped for a moment, one foot on the road, the other on the pavement. Looking around, I saw that nobody was walking close so, staring at the buildings, I decided it all looked a little like New York.

I pushed off into the traffic and wiggled up the hill at St. John's Wood Road. The big red houses gave way to smaller but still well-maintained terraces. A shift from red to brown with big white houses to my right. The air smelt heavily of money. I had no idea who owned or rented these buildings. Could one person own any of them? I wondered how many were foreign owned. Hamilton Close reminded me of a part of London time and development had left behind.

I stopped for a second, pulling the portfolio strap over my shoulder. It slipped down, pulling the scarf over my wound. The pain was instant, but instead of the usual jolt or growing ache I gagged and spat a mouthful of sick onto the beautiful cobbled street. I would have felt guilty if I knew anyone that lived there. Who lived there? I wondered. I shouted out, 'Who are you?' but no one replied. I called myself a fucking idiot and got back on the bike. I had to try to keep my mouth shut and head down. I needed to stop stopping and pissing around. I had to keep a grip on what was going on. Right now I wasn't far away from spending the rest of my life in a padded cell.

As I trundled up St John's Wood Road, muttering to myself, Lords, the home of cricket, appeared on my left. Two hundred years it had stood there watching all the comings and goings. What a different place London must have been two hundred years ago. No cars or bikes; that road would have been full of horse shit. It would have been a hell of a lot easier getting rid of a few body parts, though. But then I guess I'd have had Sherlock Holmes to deal with. Did they really play cricket and not football then?

I pondered workers playing football two hundred years ago as I manoeuvred around the tricky roundabout. As I passed by the old St John's Wood church, I looked at the cemetery. Perhaps I should stop off there and shove open an old grave and drop Mason off in there? It was a silly idea, so I rode on, undeterred, up Prince Albert Road. Even more massive, super-sized, terraced houses. I wasn't entirely sure that they weren't upmarket flats or offices. Who the fuck worked here or lived there? To the right random giant houses hid behind massive fences and guarded gated walls. It had to be homes for rich Arabs or crusty old politicians or lords or dodgy new money types. I really had no idea. Wouldn't it be nice to do a census round here? No one I knew lived here for sure.

I rode along. I was joined by Regent's Canal and its surrounding trees on my right whilst the massive flats continued unrestrained on my left, like a massive cliff face. If I was an American who lived by Central Park this is where I'd choose to live if I emigrated to London and vice versa. Why did I keep thinking of New York? New York, New York, the city that doesn't sleep. *A bit like me. God I feel tired and I'm hurting so bad. Not long now to the zoo, I've got to keep going.*

I cut through the outer part of Regent's Park on autopilot and daydreaming. I was following the bike. Squirrels everywhere with their little beady eyes boring, burning tiny holes in me. Perhaps they thought I was after their nuts. Chloe hated squirrels. They never used to bother me; in fact as a kid I used to love them. Now I hated them on principle because she did. They scared her. I felt a massive pang of bitter sadness as images of Chloe screaming and running away from scurrying squirrels whilst I laughed on a country walk years ago hounded my mind, and then my mum's face filled my head, looking at me, concerned, asking, 'What's the matter?', and then memories of my grandad's last breaths flashed through my brain. Blurred, twisted, collaged memories. As tears rolled down my cheek I rode on in a determined daze.

Gradually I picked up speed as I looked for a squirrel to run over. Circling the zoo, I couldn't find the wolves, where had they gone? They were here for *Withnail and I*. What about me? This had been a bad idea and Mr Badger hadn't done me any favours and now the squirrels looked like they might gang up to stop me nicking their nuts before they went to bed.

Trying to feed Mason to the wolves was a nuts idea. I couldn't even get that close to the railings, and even if I did manage to get a few limbs through, how on earth did I know the wolves would actually eat him? He was mostly bone for fuck's sake. I was riding around one of London's most famous parks with two stolen priceless pieces of art and one chopped-up body. I was in serious shit. I needed to get rid of the body bits and then back to the boat and get rid of the head and torso.

The protected reed beds next to the canal kept striking me as my best option, perhaps my only option. No one could get in there logically. They were protected for fuck's sake. I wonder if the RSPCB or nature programmes were allowed to film in there searching for bitterns or reed warblers. Last thing I needed was Bill Oddie sticking his beak in by stumbling across a dismembered body. No one would accidentally blunder across his body. It certainly couldn't be dug up to prepare for a housing development. You couldn't build on a protected area. Surely it would be left alone there?

Either way, standing or riding around in the park at God knows what time with a portfolio, bike and taser wasn't helping anything and I needed help.

Why does nothing ever go smoothly or at least right, once, ever? Once, at least once in a while! Where are the fucking wolves?

Part of me felt like throwing the bike on the floor, getting out the body parts and doing an impromptu and slightly morbid bring and buy sale, right there in the park, all the bits I had neatly laid out for people to browse over.

'I think I'll take the taser and the Van Gogh painting... Will you accept five pounds?'

'Certainly, sir,' I replied in my head.

Either that or I could just make a circle and sit in the middle of it and start rocking like a complete mentalist surrounded by macabre body parts. Just as I was about to start screaming 'FUCK' with all my might I noticed the warthog looking out of its enclosure right by the canal. I couldn't believe I'd ridden away from the canal to check the outside of the park to see if I could get to the wolves, when, had I stayed on the boat on the canal, I could have possibly pulled up right next to the warthog and, to my delight, the hunting dogs living next door. *That'll do nicely*, I thought.

66 – HUNTING DOGS – 7.30PM

I RODE DOWN TO THE CANAL PATH, crossing a bridge opposite the hunting dogs and the wild boar enclosure, feeling strangely euphoric. I unpacked the first satchel containing a hand and arm. I felt like I was going fishing and had just started tackling up. I thought it would be best to try a hand first rather than risk an arm. The hand was pretty black and charred. I was fairly certain it wouldn't have been possible to get any prints from the fingers.

I looked left and right to make doubly sure no one was coming. I was quite sure CCTV would be at least watching the enclosure, but whether or not there'd be someone watching twenty-four hours was relatively unknown to me. The zoo had been shut for a good few hours to the general public, but would the dogs still be hungry? I'd need to be as quick as possible. If the dogs liked the hand I'd throw the rest in sharpish and be on my way. It wasn't a massively difficult shot, but one-handed it was a different kettle of fish. My balance was screwed and I felt a little dizzy. The throw had to get over the width of the canal and be high enough to clear the fence; it was a fairly tricky shot. Normally I'd have backed myself to get ten out of ten, but I'd have to do it underarm now and really couldn't afford any cock-ups.

I stood, hand in hand, legs apart on the bank of the canal, steadying my breathing. I was shattered, paranoid and rapidly losing my confidence. What would I do if it fell in the canal or landed short on the other bank? Would it float? I looked up and down the other side. If I had to I could always swing my legs over the bridge and fall down the other side into the brambles covering the other bank. There was no path but if the worst came to the worst I could drop down or, I decided, if all else failed I could swim under the bridge. That would only be if I was really desperate, though.

I did three practice swings and on the third let go and watched the hand arc up through the sky, slowly turning and waving goodbye to me. My heart felt like it was about to explode again. It wasn't going to make it over. *It's not going to make it.* I could hear my pulse banging in my brain. I'd been too weak! Time stood still. My heart, now in my mouth, was choking me. My eyes flicked between the hand and the top of the enclosure. At the last moment it passed millimetres over the fence, barely grazing the top like a final act of stubbornness.

The dogs stood still for a moment, ears pricked and eyes wide open, locked on the new, strange, unexpected intrusion into their pen. They knew it wasn't feeding time again and yet this was an unexpected treat. A toy or perhaps food… Then, whilst the pack stood with their heads in the air, sniffing the unusual fragrance, one of the younger pooches pounced. It bolted towards the hand and grabbed it, sparking a manic race around the enclosure which suddenly became a race track that all the dogs joined in tearing around. It was instant pandemonium. Dogs chattering, scampering and excitedly yelping. They were really hungry. Perhaps they were only fed every other day and I had been lucky.

I picked up the arm, this time determined to give it some more welly and aim for the middle of the enclosure rather than giving myself another near heart attack. I set myself again on the edge of the canal with my feet fairly wide apart; as I swung the arm I caught a brief glimpse of my reflection in the brown canal water. I didn't recognise the image and didn't want to know who it was, but for a second I felt like rolling forward into the water. I shook my head clear and refocused.

It was like throwing a heavy broken branch. The arm felt slightly rubbery and yet still solid, apart from the elbow, which felt like a break in an old wooden limb. As the arm plopped down amongst the dogs with a muffled thud again the dogs momentarily froze before embarking on an almighty tug of war. They made light work of both hands and arms, but still had the main course to come. Even the wart hog had made his way snuffling out of the enclosure, looking almost dejected – why were the dogs being fed and he was missing out? I wanted to throw him a foot but wasn't sure whether he'd appreciate it.

I took the first leg out of the satchel on the bike, unwrapping it from the plastic. It was clear straightaway that the legs weighed twice as much as the arms and there was little chance I'd be able to throw these larger limbs comfortably over the canal. I threw the feet in anger like a cricketer. My bad arm burned with the frustration. I felt I had no choice but to try to get the limbs into the enclosure from the other side of the bank.

I desperately hoped I'd be able to drop down beside the bridge. It was fairly overgrown and acted like a natural barrier between the canal and the enclosure. I went round onto the bridge, looking down over the warthog pen and into the dogs. It was still too far from the bridge to attempt to throw the legs, and besides, there were large, over-hanging oak trees whose branches would act like goal-keepers, stopping me from reaching my objective. Oh fuck!

I looked either side of the bridge. The side nearest to the dogs was about a ten-foot drop and with only one arm and thick brambles on a steep bank it wasn't appealing in the slightest. Even feeling fit as a fiddle and fleeing for my life I wouldn't have chosen it as an escape route. The opposite side was more maintained, less of a drop, but the only way around the bridge was under it and there wasn't a path.

I looked up and down the canal from the middle. As far as I could see there were no signs of life. It was miserable out. Cold and wet and getting late in the day, why would anyone want to be out? I couldn't see any anyone. People would ruin everything now.

I dropped the leg over the wrong side of the bridge and ran back to the bike. I took off my coat and shoes, socks and trousers, leaning against the fence to steady myself. Nothing was easy one-handed. I picked up the last leg and wedged it under my gammy arm and trotted back to the bridge. My feet were freezing and the sticks, leaves, gravel and grass took turns biting me. Once I was back on the bridge I looked down and dropped the second leg to be reunited with the first and then climbed up on the brick bridge, looked down and dropped over. Although this side was grassier every little stick and piece of bramble dashed my ankles and legs and knees as I rolled over a few times, unable to stop myself because of my useless arm. The pain screamed at me. I scrambled to my feet, pushing myself up one-handed. It took more effort than any push-up I'd ever done in my life. I was feeling exhausted and now my arm was hurting more than it had done up to that point. I dry-wretched; I had nothing in my stomach to sick up. I gingerly went down to the edge of the canal and sat with my bloodied feet and legs dangling into the brown soup-like water. Next to me sat the other two legs.

I would have to go under the dark bridge in the water, carrying one leg at a time, before being able to get out the other side and go up the bank to get close enough to the enclosure to chuck the legs in and then be on my way. I plonked down into the freezing water. My bad arm instantly felt relieved, although my breath was taken away, and fighting to relax my breathing possibly meant I could no longer feel my arm. No matter how much I tried I couldn't catch my breath and relax. I felt like giving up. I looked at the first leg on the bank and grabbed it and forced myself on. I had to push the leg on with one hand with my bad arm in the water and use my feet on the cold, wet, weedy wall underneath me in the darkness and slime. I wondered what fish were near my feet and then wondered about eels and my bum had a strange twitch and the thought made my toes curl. I dragged myself on bit by bit under the parapet. I could only move about half a foot at a time and each movement resulted in me needing to regain my balance again before pushing on. Each time I tried to go any faster I got a face full of canal water and didn't want to drink any more than absolutely necessary and as far as I could tell I wasn't thirsty. I managed to get my breath back but was now shivering uncontrollably. It was freezing, damp, dark and squalid under the bridge; there was no path or light either side of the canal. The only things supposed to pass underneath the bridge were boats. For some reason it smelt of piss. I could hear dripping, I guessed from the road above, but the piss, I decided it might come from bats.

I dropped the first leg off and made my way back to retrieve the second. As I passed back under the bridge on my way back to the first leg I could just make out my bike on the far side of the canal with the portfolio. Someone was there. I froze and thought, *Busted, it's all over.*

All I saw was the florescent jacket and I immediately thought it was the police. But as my eyes adjusted and my initial panic subsided I could see it wasn't a policeman. I blinked, trying to focus properly. Who was it and what did they want? I thought the best thing I could do was start shouting. Hopefully it would scare whoever it was off. But the last thing I wanted to do was cause alarm or draw any attention to myself... any more than a bloke would while holding a discarded leg and wading half naked up to his neck in a canal in the freezing cold with a bloodied bullet wound in one arm. No, I really had to be careful but forceful. Fuck it; I didn't have a clue what to say. As I edged under the bridge I noticed it was a lady runner. I shouted out, 'It's okay, the bike's with me!'

It was the first thing that came into my head. It didn't occur to me that it didn't really make much sense, but it got her attention as she looked round momentarily, startled. I could see she was unsure where my voice had come from and from her body language she looked uneasy and scared as she squinted into the darkness under the bridge. I presumed she saw the ripples in the water and thought I was with the zoo or canal or bridge inspection agency or something because she jogged on, possibly worried I was a murdering nutter in the canal with somebody's body parts on a miserable Sunday night.

I waited under the bridge for a moment. I was convinced she would turn around again as she ran off and I didn't want her to see me wallowing in the canal holding a chargrilled human leg. That would look bad. I was frozen to the bone; my fingers had no sensation in them. But I held the leg and gripped the wet, slimy wall whilst my teeth did their best to make as much noise as possible by chattering away uncontrollably. As I expected, she turned round one more time before disappearing around the corner behind some hedges. I forced myself on until I got to the other leg on the bank. I hoped she hadn't noticed the bags, although she would have no conceivable way of knowing at all what was hidden in the plastic.

I put the legs together, placed my good hand on the bank and kicked with my feet to try to pull myself out of the water. I got half out but plopped back in. I tried again but couldn't even get as far as my first attempt. I slipped back into the water and took a mouthful of water. I suddenly panicked. Shit, I was stuck in the freezing canal. I searched the bank, looking for some steps. How the hell had I made such a stupid mistake? I was going to freeze to death and drown or get found and then arrested.

I frantically thrashed back towards the bridge, desperate to find some sort of way out of the canal. I was convinced the canal would be a watery end for me. There was nothing. I searched all the way to the bridge. I slapped the water in anger. The dogs in the enclosure noticed me and looked at me like I was totally mad. 'I know!' I shouted at them before I scrambled back to where I'd first started. 'Fuck!'

I went round in a desperate circle searching for some way out of the canal. I was continuously spitting water out of my mouth, looking up and down the path, hoping someone might come along, hoping I could find a way out. Then, about twenty feet away, almost level with the edge of the dogs on the other side of the canal, not far from my bike, I made out a hole in the brick wall on the bank of the canal. I swam and pulled myself along until I was level. With any luck there'd be another hole on my side of the canal as well. There was. I put one foot in the hole and pulled myself up, letting go of the bank to make a grab at the root of an old tree. It unravelled slightly but took my weight, allowing me to put some pressure on my other leg and pull myself up onto the edge.

Once up I wasted no time, I went straight to the legs, took them out of the plastic bags and tossed them one after the other straight into the enclosure. The dogs were frozen to the spot, watching me rather than the legs. I grabbed the plastic bags and ran back to the bridge. I reluctantly jumped back into the canal and swam back to the other side of the bridge through the darkness. I searched the bank for an escape route but once again couldn't see one. I took out the plastic bags and filled them with air, making a pair of inflatable air pillows. I pushed off from the wall and kicked against the current, which seemed to get stronger in the middle of the canal. I kicked my legs with all my strength but couldn't stop myself going back, further away from the bridge and the bike. I battled my way to the other side but had to pull myself along the bank under the bridge and along the canal until I reached the hole. I was pleased to see the dogs still charging around with chunks of meat. There wouldn't be much left behind in the morning, for sure.

I reached the hole, threw the empty plastic bags on the bank and finally pulled myself clear of the water. My hands were bright red but pruned. My feet and ankles were covered in small scratches. My head was banging, my nose was streaming and I had a sore throat, a dull, constant ache in my arm and itchy eyes.

I got dressed again and back on my bike. 'Bye bye, doggies,' I croaked.

67 – NCP – 9PM

I PUT THE PORTFOLIO OVER MY SHOULDER and pulled the straps as tight as possible; it couldn't hug me any tighter without me being sick. I'd shoved the empty plastic bags into the satchels on the front wheels of the bike and zipped the compartments shut. I said goodbye for the last time to the hunting dogs and hog and made my way to the steps that led up to the bridge and the path back to Regent's Park. Even though the bike was small and no longer weighed down with body parts I was knackered, and carrying it up the steps with one arm and a massive portfolio on my back proved simply impossible. I held the handlebars at arm's length and gradually bumped the bike each step of the way; unfortunately every step sent wild reverberations through my body, causing pulses of nausea to whirl through my gut. My nose was now running freely, but because I only had one hand and that was pushing the bike I had no choice but to sniff constantly in a losing battle, trying to ebb the relentless flow of snot. I lost the battle and war by the time I got to the top of the stairs. Attractively, I had a trail of slime all the way past my mouth and chin and onto my jacket. I placed the bike up against the wall and wiped my mouth and nose on my sleeve. I must have been ten years old since I'd done that last. I felt physically sick and needed to warm up as quickly as possible. I tried to clear my throat but it burnt to buggery. I needed a pack of Strepsils and a pack of Beechams and to at least soak my arm in salty water and apply some new bandages. I wanted a hot bath, or better still to be a Roman solider pampered by beautiful maids doused in exotic flagrancies. God only knew what I looked like.

I put my leg over the frame of the bike and, using my good arm, placed my duff hand on the handlebars. I couldn't move my fingers and definitely couldn't use the brake but my thumb felt a tiny bit more responsive and although it burnt the whole way up my arm I could just about hold on to the grip. I turned both the front and back lights on and made my way alongside the Regent's Park outer ring towards Marylebone Road. It was getting darker.

Even if I wanted to go any faster the portfolio acted like an umbrella. The blustery wind couldn't make up its mind whether it was going to help or hinder me. One minute it pushed me back, then it pushed me on and I didn't need to pedal, and then it tried to push me off. I took it slowly; I certainly wouldn't be racing any couriers on single-geared racers today.

I got to Marylebone Road and panicked when I saw the traffic. It was insane. Regent's Park had virtually been deserted save a few dog walkers, runners, weirdos and stranger tourists, but there had been no traffic. Even the squirrels on guard had let me pass. Marylebone Road was different, though; it seemed mental. It was alive, a heaving mass of vehicles and moving metal all angry and wanting to be somewhere else. Everything and everyone was late already. Everyone was on a mission. Everything was dazzling: the noise, the lights, the indicators, the car horns, the loud motorbikes. It was like Silverstone and I was a hedgehog or carthorse, slug or sloth. I was going to die.

I didn't want the lights to change. I wanted them to stay red forever. I really didn't fancy joining the traffic. It felt like you do when you're about to jump in the sea or the pool when you're on a really hot holiday. I felt sick and gagged again. The lights changed and a car I hadn't noticed bibbed me. I looked round to wave them on but they were already passing me. I muttered under my breath and pushed off, wobbling into a left-hand turn that led straight into another set of traffic lights. The car that had just overtaken me was a silver Mercedes with tinted windows. It had a strange personalised number plate that read UCI 8U. I stood behind it with one foot on the curb, trying to work out what on earth it meant. Did it mean 'hate' or 'ate'? I wasn't sure which was worse, and I stopped contemplating when a stream of traffic joined us shortly before the lights changed again and I carefully made my way past Great Portland Street on my right and a big old church on my left.

I had a stream of cars go past me and each felt too close, like they were invading my space, and as I made my way into the bus lane and away from the constant moving blockade a poxy bendy bus cruised up right behind me. The driver didn't have enough time to overtake me before the next stop and there was already another bendy bus sitting at the stop anyway. The driver couldn't have got any closer to the back of me if he tried. If I fell off the bike now he would undoubtedly drive straight over me or drag me along, pinned by the portfolio, grated into the road. I concentrated on keeping the bike steady whilst continually checking the road ahead. I would have loved to have stuck two fingers up at him but couldn't take a hand off the handlebars. If I tried to look behind the bike wobbled wildly. I had no choice but to keep focused on what was in front of me. Forget all the traffic whizzing around me. I had to stop behind the bus already pulled over as there was no way I could overtake with the big portfolio on my back.

I pulled up behind the bus to bide my time and turned round to look at the inconsiderate bus driver. He looked like Robert Mugabe but I couldn't get him to look at me. It wasn't like I could or would do anything anyway, I just wanted to give him a dirty look and possibly call him a prick. I was quite sure he got called that and worse every single day. Whilst I waited for the bus to pull away I decided bus drivers hated the taxi drivers who hated the motorists who hated the cyclists who hated the pedestrians. Then I decided everyone hated everyone, and right then everyone hated me.

The bus pulled away and I followed at a decent distance, all the while keeping in the bus lane and away from the faster traffic. Even the Boris bikes raced past me. Down Marylebone Road I went, past Euston and the British Library, concentrating on keeping steady. I pulled up level with King's Cross. I had no choice: I'd have to get out of the bus lane soon as a constant stream of buses pulling in would end up cutting me up. The only way out was to gain some momentum.

I dropped a couple of cogs and immediately it felt like my legs were no longer moving. Shifting all my weight from leg to leg, I gradually picked up some speed. I couldn't indicate and simply had to trust whoever was in the lane next to me wasn't too busy on the phone or smoking a fag or changing the radio or applying make-up or looking at bogies up their nostrils. As the next car drew level and began to pass me I edged out as closely as possible to their rear tail lights. I was riding along the thick red line that marked the border of the bus lane.

The stationary bus then decided to pull away just as I pulled out to overtake. He hadn't indicated or even looked in his mirrors. I panicked as the portfolio on my left-hand side felt like it was on a direct collision course with the bus, but I couldn't pull out any more because the car beside me was now slowing down and the two vehicles were squeezing me tighter and tighter into a vanishing gap. I squeezed my brakes as hard as I could and braced myself for the searing pain that would inevitably scream up my arm like it had every time I'd tried to use the brakes so far. My right arm struggled to compensate for my left. I felt the weight of the pictures and portfolio pushing me forward. I couldn't slow down fast enough. No matter how hard I squeezed the brakes, I couldn't stop.

The bus hissed to a halt and the car slowed to a crawl. I aimed the front wheel of the bike into the little space between the car and the bus whilst my eyes flicked between them and my white knuckles. The car pulled away as my portfolio clattered on the side of the bus. My bike swung in as well and the handlebars jolted my hands free and disappeared to the floor. I raised one hand to stop my face hitting the bus although the portfolio's momentum checked me and my feet lost the pedals and wrestled with the floor to stay flat. My legs lost the fight and the pedals swung round and bit my right shin in a final act of stubborn nastiness. 'FUCK!' My leg hurt like someone had hit it with an axe. I held my head on the bus for a second before bending down to pick up the bike.

I watched as the bus driver nonchalantly adjusted his mirror to see what was going on near the rear of his vehicle. I waved a hand as if to say it was okay and he tapped his head as if to say I wasn't so I went into a dickhead hand gesture and he pulled away again, leaving me standing in the middle of the street. This somehow seemed to give me some more space and I was able to ride on although I was desperate to stop and look at my shin. I could imagine the blue bruise and dots of blood and torn skin.

The traffic was being held at the lights behind me so I left King's Cross and the *Big Issue* seller mumbling 'Pig tissue' and made my way up the steep hill of Pentonville Road. The cycle path there was tiny with so many buses and it was such a steep hill I felt my weaving and dodgy riding would be better and safer on the pavement; as long as I didn't see any overzealous policeman or traffic wardens, I should be alright. I weaved around drains, signposts and bus stops and bumped up and down curbs. I was in the highest gear possible and although my legs were moving ten to the dozen I wasn't getting anywhere fast. I was sweating but didn't feel hot. I was puffing through my arse.

When I got to the top of the hill I cut up Baron Street. At the end of the road I went right at Chapel Market. Manzes Pie and Mash shop called out to me far more than The Alma pub. I didn't think I'd look out of place in either establishment, but as much as I could do with food and beer I wanted to get the hell out of London and didn't feel like stopping. I rode through the Sainsbury's car park, past The Angelic pub on Liverpool Road and then into the NCP car park next to the Islington Design Centre on Upper Street. I plunged down one level and found the old BMW where I had left it on Friday morning. I took the portfolio off my shoulder and stuck it in the boot. I folded up the bike and put that on the back seat. I got into the driver's seat, turned on the engine and put the heating on full power.

68 – NOT DESMOND TUTU – 9PM–9AM

I WOKE UP TO HEAR THE TAPPING against the window. I blinked sleepily at my reflection to see a big round African face looking in at me with bright white teeth, scowling ferociously.

'What are you doing?' the Nigerian face demanded.

'I fell asleep,' I said wearily as I opened the window a crack.

'You cannot sleep here,' he barked. 'This isn't a drive through hotel, you know.'

'I know, I know, I just fell asleep. I'm going now,' I said, leaning forward to check the dashboard for the parking ticket.

'You cannot pay with cash,' he added.

I must have turned the engine off before falling asleep. Why couldn't I pay with cash?

'You what?' I replied.

'It's card only, okay, card only. The machine is not accepting cash at the moment, I think the bloody Europeans... you know... have been tampering again with the bloody machine, okay.' He sucked his teeth and looked at me a little more closely. 'What is wrong with your arm and your face?'

'Nothing,' I said.

I was beyond sick of the nosy car park attendant. Perhaps I should zap him, stick him in the boot and set the car on fire? I did up the window to end the conversation and waved away the strangely orange face. I pulled down the sun visor and the parking ticket fell out. It fluttered past my flapping hand too quickly for me to react and catch it and yet still in slow motion enough for me to appreciate its ebb and flow. I cursed as it settled between my feet and I had to pull my seat back to be able to get my head under the steering wheel and reach between my legs to get the ticket. As the air was forced from my lungs I panicked for a second, thinking I was

180

stuck like that, head between legs under the steering wheel. I'd heard stories of couples caught in compromising positions whilst in the midst of making love and didn't like the idea of becoming another story for the fireman to be discussing in the future.

I nudged the ticket annoyingly further away so I had to abandon my attempt and get out of the car to reach it. The cold blast of damp underground air went right through me and I felt like I'd been slapped round the face and suddenly brought to my senses; because I remembered I still hadn't paid for the car park. I walked towards the machine, one hand hanging useless by my side. My head was spinning again. I felt like I was walking on an uneven floor. Was my arm dragging me off kilter? I looked back at the car to make sure it wasn't at a funny angle and then back at the ticket machine. I noticed the nosy car park attendant in his little office put down a clipboard and stop what he was doing to watch me more closely. I was the monkey in the zoo. I tried to ignore him and patted my pocket as if I was just thinking I'd left the ticket in the car and reassuring myself. I knew it was in my hand; he didn't.

I got to the machine and slid the ticket in. It reluctantly stuttered and grabbed it from me and then calculated I owed it forty-seven pounds twenty, so I paid from our joint account and waited for it to spit back my ticket and card. The NCP guy came out of his little office to check my payment was successful; he looked almost gutted when the transaction was complete. I figured he'd already planned how he'd take me down and bust me up whilst waiting for the authorities. I laughed at him and said, 'See you later.' I wouldn't be returning. This guy was on me like a hawk.

I walked back to the car, put the ticket on the dashboard within easy reach and concentrated for a second, trying to work out how I was going to drive a manual car one-handed. I had no choice, but the only way it would be possible was going to be changing gear as little as possible. Turning the big old BMW was going to be hard enough one-handed, but changing gear would mean using my knees on the steering wheels and leaning across myself to reach the gear stick. I tried to swallow but my mouth was bone dry. I had to think hard to remember how to drive at all. I started to doubt myself and remembered the nosy attendant who would be gawping at me from his little office. I put the key in the ignition and turned but nothing happened. The car sounded like a heavy smoker rattling in the morning. It coughed and spluttered but just wouldn't bite. 'Fuck it,' I shouted and punched the steering wheel with my good hand. I should never have come to the car. I looked out of the window half-expecting to see the attendant laughing or striding over with knuckle dusters gleaming in the Jaffa-orange light. I couldn't see him anywhere; perhaps he was on the phone to the cops.

I leant across the passenger seat and opened the glove box. Inside there was a can of Quick Start. If this didn't work I'd have to leave the car and continue on my bike, maybe just go straight back to the boat. 'Shit.' I didn't know what to do. I went round the front of the car and opened the bonnet. I had to do it like a one-handed weight lifter. Why was everything proving so difficult? I couldn't work out if it was because I was invalided or because I was unlucky. Would things be conspiring against me and taking so long if I could use two hands, or was this because of karma? I didn't know. What I did know was that the sick feeling was returning and my head was pounding and the fumes from the spray had burnt my already sore throat as I sprayed the hose that ran towards the engine. I dropped the bonnet down, and threw the can on the passenger seat. Got back in the car, counted to ten, had a dab, dropped a pill, necked a bomb and partied on… Counted to ten, had a dab, necked a pill, dropped a bomb and partied on.

I sat in the driver's seat. I put my crap arm and hand on my lap. The steady burn was a constant reminder, never comforting, just acting like a brooding, angry volcano, and each time I moved sending a searing, molten pain erupting from my swollen fingers through my hand past my wrist and elbow and then intensifying like a million miniature explosions ripping up towards my shoulder. I wasn't sure if it was better hanging by my side or if I should have tried to make some sort of sling. It hadn't felt this bad before I went to sleep and I was sure it was gradually getting worse. What was gradually? How long ago had I been shot? Had I really been shot? All this wasn't just a nightmare? I had hoped that it wasn't that bad but it hadn't really stopped bleeding and no matter how hard I tried I couldn't move my fingers. I had wiped the blood off my hand and been in the water, and the riding must have made it bleed more heavily; that would possibly explain why I kept having massive waves of tiredness.

I wasn't sure how long I'd been asleep in the car before being woken. The old clock in the car had stopped working years ago, though I guessed mathematically there was a chance it could be right. What should I expect outside? Light or dark? I could sleep now. Just a few minutes more. I went to check my watch but it was on my bad arm and the pain of moving it outweighed my curiosity about the time. What happened if I got to Spaces and it was shut? How long had the boat been left moored up? Would Mason's head and body still be submerged with the anchor?

I'd been a massive fool. I shouldn't have taken the pictures with me on the bike. I should have left them on the boat and got them in the car at another time. Would it have been worth leaving them on the boat, though? Surely that would have been more risky? Why was I determined to doubt myself? I had to get a move on. What was done was done and I had to find out if I could drive one-handed before worrying about doing things differently.

I put the key in the ignition and said a little prayer that the Quick Start spray had worked its magic. The engine bit immediately and roared to life, kicking out a huge plume of grey smoke. She was alive. I put my foot on the clutch, and lent over myself like I was wiping my bum with my right hand although going in from the left-hand cheek direction. I got the gear into reverse by pushing down on the stick and slowly turned the wheel as the car gradually crept backwards. I could steer using my palm; my early Essex boy intense driving training would come in handy after all. I crossed myself again to put the gear into first. Steering wasn't going to be a problem, I reassured myself; but changing gears was going to be a nightmare. I crunched and made a song and dance of finding first gear. I thought I'd found it and the gear slipped into neutral. I tried a second time, feeling a nervous apprehension setting in: if I didn't find it now I would begin to panic. It went in and I pulled away from the car space and made my way past the office, through the gate and up the ramp. All in first gear and relatively easy.

I was sweating again and my head was pounding. It was light out. I must have been asleep right through the night. It was possible I'd only slept for five minutes but it looked too bright

69 – ONE ARMED BANDIT

I PULLED INTO THE FIRST LIGHT of my day and immediately felt like a racing driver on the starting grid waiting for the green lights to change. As soon as I was sure the road was clear to the right I swung the old BMW out onto the road. As the car accelerated and I felt the inevitable need to change gear I was saved by another set of traffic lights. As always, the traffic in Islington was fairly heavy and the chances were I wasn't likely to manage much more speed than I had achieved on my bike. But with the heat from the engine warming me and the nauseous taste in my throat momentarily subsiding I hit the radio, XFM, and turned it up. Queens of the Stone Age – 'No One Knows'. I wondered how true that was. Perhaps the sultan's house was crawling with police and inspectors right now. Perhaps Mason's head and torso had been found anchored off the boat or his hands and feet partly consumed at London Zoo. The boat had been traced to Chloe's parents. They would surely be close to having me as the number one suspect.

My mind drifted and the baseline pounded my brain. I fell into a semi-conscious state, daydreaming. This was rudely interrupted by the flashing lights and honking horn from the car behind me. I jumped on the accelerator and tried to flash my indicators left and right as a way of an apology. This was a waste of time as unlike country folk the city types would just presume I intended to turn left and then right. I'd also noticed city drivers use their hazard lights as indicators in past. All it indicated to me was that the driver felt like he or she had right of way over every other driver. It really wasn't worth being kind or considerate whilst driving in London. If you let someone out or in they never said thank you. People were very quick to flash or beep you. London wasn't not the place to drive if you weren't an aggressive driver. Londoners were hard, insular types. Murderers even.

The time came to change gear. I put my foot on the accelerator, raised one knee to rest my leg on the steering wheel and reached across myself to change into second gear. Getting out of first was easy, but as the car coasted on, slightly drifting to the left, the need to turn to the right became more apparent, and as the gears crunched and as my eyes desperately checked the gear layout I realised I had been trying to select reverse. With the curb only inches away I found second and hastily took my hand from the gear stick to the steering wheel and veered right, swerving like a lady putting on her slap or a bloke answering his phone discreetly. I was spared the rigmarole of having to change up to third gear by another set of traffic lights at the bottom of Upper Street in Islington. I undid the window, trying to get some air into the rapidly sweltering car. I dry-wretched as I inhaled fresh exhaust from a black cab beside me. My lips felt chapped and dry; bits of dry skin jutted off them. Licking them just made them burn more. I put the car back into first and tried to read the road in an attempt to pre-empt any gear changes or difficult steering manoeuvres that were going to soon become obstacles.

I still didn't know what the time was... Would Spaces be open? I checked the rear-view mirror, suddenly paranoid I was being watched. I was sure I was going to turn and see a police car. I felt like someone was sitting behind me in the car. Sitting on my shoulder and staring into my ear. I tried to look behind me in the car. I even looked up at the roof to make sure no one was looking down on me. I was going mad. I was alone. No one was watching me, until a young Asian girl in the car in the next lane pulled up level with me. Her parents seemed oblivious to the murdering nutter sitting a few feet from their precious daughter, but she knew I wasn't right. Was it because I was talking to myself? 'Is it?' I shouted at her. Her big brown eyes just burnt a hole into my soul. The little Pocahontas had my number. I stuck out my tongue, blinked and looked away. I didn't fancy my chances in a staring competition. As soon as the lights changed I beeped my car's horn at the dithering driver in front and edged forward, breaking the little witch's spell.

70 – SPACE INVADER

I BUNDLED THROUGH THE DOORS OF SPACES to see Georgee Paris sitting staring, baffled, back at me. There were no customers milling around; there never really were that many at Spaces. He spent most of his day reading about West Ham on the internet. People tended to come by to drop off stuff and go about their lives, happy in the knowledge their belongings were someone else's responsibility.

'Jesus, mate, you look a right two and eight,' he said.

'I've felt better,' I replied, slumping into the blue plastic chair opposite him. 'I need your help,' I said frankly. My voice was a dry rasp.

'No problem, mate, what is it? What happened to your lip and you're head? Has someone smacked you? Who was it?'

'Can I have water, please?'

He got up and made me a cup. The bubbles rippled up through the translucent blue container.

Georgee was a legend. I'd met up with him at West Ham a fair few times. We moved in different circles but were still very good mates. I assumed he thought I was going to ask him to look after something hot. Put something stolen into storage. That was all those places were good for after all; lock-ups for valuables people hadn't quite worked out how or where to leave at home.

Georgee had seen the lot and could deal with most things. I had heard he was a bit of a nutter, although I had never witnessed it first-hand. There was a story of him getting arrested for running onto the football pitch trying to get to the away support. After being dragged away by the police and stewards he'd been placed in the holding cells in the basement of West Ham, which I always imagined to resemble an old-fashion barred prison. He'd made some rival fans cry, not by saying anything in particular but by continuously staring at them in the separate cell and continuously growling and head-butting the bars over and over again.

I took a mouthful of water and began. 'Georgee, do you want my car?'

'Why, don't you want it? How much do you want for it? Where'd you get it from?'

Why ask one question when you can ask three? I thought.

'Look, mate, I haven't got time to explain. I have all the documents, you can do what you like with it, and I haven't got the space for it at home and can't drive it home now anyway. I need to drop a few bits and bobs off now with you but after that you can do what you like with the car, okay? I don't want it, I want you to have it. Do what you like with it,' I said with as much sincerity as I could muster.

'Okay, mate, you can leave it out the front of the shop where it is now. Give me the keys and I'll park it in a moment. I'll sort you out later for it. Jeez Louise what have you done to your arm, mate? You look really ill – what on earth have you been up to?'

'I've not been up to anything. Even if I had I couldn't tell you anything. Please don't ask me any more. Can you also forget you've seen me today and that I've left anything here?'

'Who are you?' Georgee said with smiling eyes. He went on: 'Let me at least order you a cab home, eh? Do you need any money; you look like you've been sleeping rough or in the car or something. Do you want a beer? How about that cab...'

'No, no cab, no beer, no nothing. I don't want anyone else knowing I've been here and I can't afford to get comfy or be seen in any cabs or early morning bars. No, thank you anyway. I'll just drink my drink, drop off a few bits and you can forget you ever saw me today, right? I'll be back and we can have a catch up then. Just let me get on my way, mate.'

'You must be in trouble? Is this about Chloe?'

Her name smacked me round the face like a sledgehammer.

'Georgee, please, mate! No, I can't talk now. I'm going to get out of your way. Thanks for taking the car.'

I pushed myself up from the table and made my way back to the car. Of course it was about Chloe. Everything was about Chloe. I took out the paperwork, bike and portfolio. I was becoming used to only using one hand. I carried the portfolio back into Spaces and made my way to my allotted spot. After dropping off the portfolio I walked back to the reception where Georgee was staring out of the window drinking a coffee out of a massive claret and blue West Ham mug. The smell wafting around the airy office made me feel sick and my stomach did a somersault.

'Are you sure I can't help you with anything?' Georgee said.

'No, not really,' I replied. I knew he cared but didn't care that he did.

'Here's the vehicle registration details and all the necessary paperwork; it's all signed, you just need to add your details and send it off. I was going to give it to the fire brigade so honestly if you want it and can take it do whatever you like with it, no strings.'

'You'd best be careful, you nutter!' Georgee said.

'And get yourself cleaned up, you look a bleedin mess'

'Love you, Georgee,' I replied.

'Shut up, you mug,' he said warmly.

With a half-hearted wave I made my way back to the bike. As much as I didn't fancy riding any more I knew it was downhill most of the way and I really was on my way home now. I needed to get a move on: the boat had to get back safely before anyone noticed it had been gone for any serious length of time, and I still had to work out what to do with Mason's head and body.

71 – THE LIGHT

ONCE I'D MOORED THE BOAT BACK UP outside the house and made sure it was as clean as when I'd taken it I covered it again and went back into Chloe's parents' house. I was quite sure the boat wouldn't be used any time soon. Chances were Chloe's dad would never use it again.

As I walked through the house I noticed the condolence cards on the windowsills and covering most surface areas. Already gathering dust. An old red rose lay on the sideboard, withered; I recognised it from the funeral. I couldn't look at the cards or the flowers. They cut me to the core like an icy sword.

In the empty house there were two expensive-looking pictures hung in modern-looking frames opposite two elegant, old-fashioned-style frames encasing a mounted West Ham shirt and also a piece of artwork by an unknown art student. One day someone would recognize the expensive-looking pictures, but believe them to be no more than unbelievable copies of real works of art. No one was at home, though there was a blood-stained blue scarf in the bin and newspapers on the coffee table were open to a report of a break-in and of a missing person at a famous sultan's house.

Initial reports suggested an inside job and the police were eager to speak to the weekend watchman who was believed to be on the run and was the chief suspect in the theft of two missing pictures believed to be original priceless works of art. One was uninsured and the other was originally stolen, acquired on the black market but that wasn't mentioned in the article. The papers sat next to an older newspaper open on the obituary pages. A young woman had died whilst in childbirth. My wife and baby were gone. The house echoed with deserted enchantment. The heating was off and everywhere felt cold. The pilot light had gone out.